Benjamin Manry

AND THE

Crimson Journal

BOOK TWO
of

The Adventures of
Benjamin Manry

BENJAMIN MANRY

AND THE

Crimson Journal

Owen Palmiotti

Benjamin Manry and the Crimson Journal

Copyright © 2011 Owen Palmiotti. All rights reserved. No part of this book may be reproduced or retransmitted in any form or by any means without the written permission of the publisher.

Published by Wheatmark®
610 East Delano Street, Suite 104, Tucson, Arizona 85705 U.S.A.
www.wheatmark.com

ISBN: 978-1-60494-542-3
LCCN: 2010940646

"You make your own destiny."

-Blood Bones-

To the
Cadets, Crew, and
Officers of the TSES,
Enjoy!

There are a lot of people that help you through writing a book. For me, I'd like to express my gratitude to the memory of my mother, Lorraine Palmiotti. This also goes out to my friends and family for their support over the years, to Lynne for doing an excellent job with the editing, to Ellibi for her support throughout the manuscript. Also, I express my utmost thanks to the friendly personnel at Wheatmark for getting my words in print. And lastly, to the readers who make a writer enjoy their job of putting their thoughts down on paper, because after all, without you guys, I wouldn't be writing this dedication.

Enjoy!

1

June 8, 1763
Somewhere in the Atlantic Ocean

Benjamin Manry tossed and turned throughout the night. When he finally awoke from the incessant nightmares, his face was covered with sweat. He heard the tolling of a bell aboard the HMS *Courtesy* and the steady footfalls of the watch making rounds about the vessel. It was only three in the morning, and an hour before he had to stand watch. He shrugged; it was pointless to attempt sleep now. Ben sat up from the bed and moved to his desk. He lit the oil lamp that hung from the overhead and then pulled open the top drawer to remove his journal. Leafing through the old entries, he found a blank page. His fingers quickly found the ink jar and a quill, eager to unite pen and paper to ease his mind.

June 8, 1763

It's been almost a week since we've set sail from Boston. A large crowd saw us off, cheering for our successful mission. It was there where we left the fearless pirate Blood Bones and his men swaying from the gallows. King George III gave us orders to find the location of, and then raid the secret lair that was home to hundreds of pirates that plagued the waters along the coasts of the Colonies.

We are now on our eastward journey to London for our next mission. So far the wind has been favorable and the seas calm. Sal and Harris were ecstatic when they saw the treasure chests below deck as we left the harbor. Captain Nelson said that they contain our wages for the past mission, as well as for the upcoming mission. I'm under the impression that this can only mean something dangerous and extremely important. I am looking forward to it as we slowly inch our way across the chart to our destination.

With my recent promotion to first officer aboard the HMS Courtesy, I stand the watch of my choosing. The four to eight is my favorite, as I am able to see a celestial dance of stars, the moon, and the sun, twice in a single day. Staring at these gifts from God, I sit and ponder my existence here on Earth. What is my destiny? Why did the curse of Blood Bones send me back in time to 1763? Why did it have to happen to me?

Of course, I must also think of my brother Harris, and our best friend Sal, since they were with me when we discovered the cursed treasure of Blood Bones. We planned a typical weekend trip of hiking, canoeing, and exploring Roosevelt Island, but the adventure that ensued was, and still continues to be, much more exciting than our wildest imaginations could have dreamt up.

We came to the year 1763 as time-travelers, cursed through the perils of time, floating on a chest in the warm waters of the Caribbean. We climbed up the anchor chain of an English flagged schooner. I remember the curves and lines of the vessel Frendrich. She was beautiful. I say was, because later on in our adventure, we shipwrecked on an uncharted island in a horrible storm. But, that is many months from where my story begins.

Shortly after the three of us joined forces with Captain Arthur F. Nelson, we had an intense sea battle against El

Perro Loco. After we won the fight, we pulled into the harbor of Grand Bahama to repair the damage to our ship, as well as begin readying for the mission to capture Blood Bones and his men. The pirate captain was hunted by every European seafaring nation that had colonies in the New World.

We then hired on a bunch of sailors for the upcoming mission, as well as a reputable carpenter to help refit. His son, Jacob, is our age and is the fourth musketeer in our group. We hang out all the time, talking about life, liberty, and the pursuit of all things awesome. It was here on this lovely island where I gave my heart away for the first time of my life. I fell in love with Leah Williamson. She's the governor's daughter and is the most beautiful person my eyes have ever gazed upon.

We then embarked on our mission to Havana, Cuba where we were to question several captured men of Blood Bones. A few days out of the Bahamas, we sailed right into a storm that pounded our ship to pieces, literally. This is where our misfortunes began. After the Frendrich was pushed far off course, we faltered on a rock and the vessel basically split in half. Those who managed to survive found safety on the island, those who didn't, lost their lives in the churning water. We built new homes for ourselves and hunted and gathered like the primitive man of our ancestry. It was such an adrenaline rush to be living off the land.

We lived on this island for several months and during that time befriended a local tribe called the Iraja that was in the midst of a war with another tribe. Through an interpreter, we learned of their constant warring, and discovered a beneficial opportunity. In exchange for our help against their enemy, they would help us off the island to continue our journey to Havana.

We battled the Hetra, and after our victory, a few

Irajan warriors guided us in dugout canoes between several islands of the Caribbean. When we finally got to Cuba, we interrogated several pirates associated with Blood Bones. We learned of the location of his secret lair, and successfully laid siege to his island hideout. From there we sailed to Boston for the hearings and the hangings of the pirates.

That is just the summed up version of my tale. I truly have had the adventure of a lifetime, but it saddens me sometimes at the same time. I say that because I left a boring and common life behind. I am from the future, not the eighteenth century. My life has changed in so many ways. I wonder if it's even possible to travel back forward through space and time so I could return home. I'd be back to my boring life in St. Augustine, back to my loving parents, my amazing friends, and all that I miss dear.

But to be honest, I wonder if I'd even want to go back now. I've thought about it so much. I am young and successful, sailing as first officer aboard a beautiful ship and serving one of the most reputable men I've ever known. Back home, I was just a kid who got good grades in school, and had a tight group of friends that would go on weekend adventures together. The ironic thing is that my friends are here with me in the past and my weekend adventures are now life-long!

By word of mouth passed on down over the years, only one man built the Manry family estate in 1778. This means that something will happen to Harris, or perhaps even to myself. To know that something might happen to him is a very scary feeling. He's my brother and we've become so close and have come so far in the last few months. Though it's only 1763 and fifteen years will transpire before my family's estate is built, I'll get to see the Revolutionary War with my own eyes, rather than reading about it in history books. I wonder where I'll be when it starts and what I'll be doing with my life. If I continue to serve Captain Nelson, maybe I'll even serve in the war as well, but as a British officer or an American, I know not. I am very excited at the prospect of traveling the world in one of the most important times of early American history, but even more exciting, is the fact I'll be a part of it. Maybe I'll even be a key figure! The possibilities are endless and that just makes me smile.

I often wonder how my family is doing back at the house. I think of my other friends back at school sometimes, but I mostly think of my parents. Ma's probably standing at the door waiting with her arms crossed across her chest, while dad's smiling, knowing that I had this coming. I would always ask the question what if. Well, what if became what is, and now I'm living in my wildest dreams and fantasies. So theoretically, you could say I got what I wished for.

BM

2

**Present Day
Roosevelt Island
St. Augustine, Florida**

The sun momentarily blinded the group of six as they emerged from the dark and musty cave system. Two policemen led the four parents on an unsuccessful quest to find their missing children. The group navigated through a maze of tangled paths that would eventually take them back to a small police motorboat. Linda Draben remained at a loss for words walking beside her husband. She gripped the cursed staff of Blood Bones close to her body with white knuckles, knowing that the object was part of the reason that her son and his two best friends had been unexpectedly taken away.

The group stepped onto the beach, leaving the sullen woods behind. Mother's instinct caused both females to look back, hoping their children were just playing a joke on them and would all of a sudden come running from the wooded edge. But no one did. The woods remained dreary, as if taunting them.

John Manry looked around the beach, scanning for anything out of place. He thought he had remembered seeing a canoe tied to a tree inside the inlet, but soon discovered nothing but an occasional set of stray footprints and some marks in the sand. John paused and gave his wife's hand a reassuring squeeze. They watched as the policemen dragged their boat to the water's edge. As the parents boarded the boat, Bill held the gunwale steady while his fellow officer, Tom, primed the small outboard engine. With a few pulls, it roared to life. Tom sat at the wheel while Bill pushed off.

The boat motored across the watery expanse to where the police launch was located. It was a quiet ride as each delved into thought. They were hesitant to share their views on the bizarre scenes that they had just stumbled upon, things no parent should ever have to witness. Their children were lost to the perils of time, cursed to a life in 1763.

Soon the boat touched the pier and Tom stood with his hand extended, helping the distressed parents one by one off the boat.

Bill looked at his watch and then grabbed at the walkie-talkie on his hip. "Base One, this is Officer Eight. En route to Home Base."

There was a static pause, and then a weak voice came in. "This is Base One. Roger that, Officer Eight. See you shortly."

✖✖✖

Tom extracted three missing person forms from a tabbed manila folder and placed them beside his keyboard. He took a sip of the black coffee and then closed his eyes. For a split second he let the aroma of the freshly brewed drink calm his nerves. He knew it would be a long and difficult evening, perhaps one of his worst, since he personally knew the boys involved. He held back a sigh to maintain his composure in front of the parents.

"John, Margie." He paused and then looked at the other couple, "Jorge, Linda, this is what I am thinking. I am convinced your children stumbled upon something on that cursed island. I've lived here my whole life and I even ventured out there as a kid. I knew your boys very well; they are good kids."

The parents nodded. "Yeah, they are," John Manry chimed in.

"Well, the point I'm trying to make is that they wouldn't fake their deaths or run away. They weren't pranksters." Tom stopped for a moment to take another sip of coffee. "Something definitely happened to your boys, as much as I hate to say that. To what extent,

I'm not sure, but I can promise you that I'm going to find out what it is. You have my word. I'll do some more digging around tomorrow morning at sunup when there's more light." Tom coughed into a napkin. "Excuse me for that. As I was saying, Michael Yocklem, my roommate from college, is a specialist in eighteenth-century weaponry and nautical relics at the Boston Museum in Massachusetts; maybe he can give some insight into all of this. I know for a fact he will definitely help out if he can. Linda, you have the staff and that written note, right?"

"Yes, I do." She placed the two objects on the table so all could see.

"So you think we should send this cursed staff and note to him?" Jorge Draben looked down at the objects.

"Yeah, I do." Tom paused. "I would like to search the island again with a few more set of eyes. Between the island and the cave system, we should have it thoroughly searched within a few days. We'll leave the dirty stuff to my guys, but I would rather have a professional look at the staff and the note. The curse of Blood Bones is well known in the nautical world. The best thing is to just search the island as best we can and see if anything comes up in our efforts. In the meantime, we can put up a few fliers here and there in town."

John shifted his weight in the seat, eager to add his own opinion. "Tom, you're right. We don't even know how this thing works, or even how our kids opened it. Look, this piece of paper obviously came from inside the cursed staff, but even if we were to figure out how to pry it open again without breaking it, we're still behind on everything. It looks to me that it is an important piece of the puzzle. If we damaged the staff they could be lost forever. We just have to keep our finger's crossed and hope we find something in the next few days."

His point seemed to convince all around the table.

Linda sighed. "Well, I kind of wanted to keep the staff, you know, in the off-chance that they would return."

Margie placed a comforting hand on her best friend's arm. "Don't worry, Linda. Our children are smart; they'll find a way back. I'm sure of it. Trust me."

John smiled at his wife's confidence in the situation. "Well, I think we're settled then." He turned to the police officer. "Let's contact your friend and send him this."

"Okay, I'm glad all parties agree," Tom said. He wrote an address down on a piece of paper. "Try and mail it out as soon as possible."

✖✖✖

Dear Mr. and Mrs. Manry,

I regret that your family has had to go through such a tragic event. It plagues me how God chooses our fates. But this is not a letter about fate or religion, so I will get to the point. Please have the aforementioned staff wrapped for a pickup tomorrow at noon. I have dispatched a UPS truck to arrive at your residence at the appropriate time. Again, I express my sympathy for your loss.

Professor Michael D. Yocklem
Curator of Nautical Finds, Boston Museum, MA

John Manry placed the letter back in its envelope and sighed loudly. "Margie, the UPS truck will be here any minute now, can you do me a favor and get a box from the closet?"

"Of course honey."

The two worked together at assembling the box. John held the staff while his wife took several sheets of newspaper and wrapped the cursed staff. She then carefully placed the staff into the confines and protection of several millimeters of cardboard. She gripped a roll of tape and pulled off several long lengths, handing them to her husband. The box was now taped to ensure its safety for the trip to Boston, Massachusetts.

✖✖✖

*P*rofessor Yocklem heard a knock on his office door. "Yes, yes, come in."

The UPS deliveryman entered the room carrying a long box in the crook of an elbow. "There you are. If you'd just sign here," he said, pointing to a screen display on a handheld scanner.

The professor gripped the tech pen and scribbled his name. "Thank you," he said as the man gave him the package.

Retreating back to his desk, he wiped off several crumbs from a doughnut he had eaten earlier with a napkin. He then scrubbed at a coffee ring that reflected the light from the ceiling. He peeled layer after layer of tape off the box. Finally the cardboard gave way, revealing the beautiful staff. His fingers moved across its surface, probing at all angles for the secret notch that had closed once the boys had read the cursed message.

After hours of meticulous studying with a large magnifying glass, the objects yielded no further information. The staff seemed to glow as if mocking him, but the rolled message at least gave him something to work with. When his lab assistant brought the radiocarbon dating results, the data indicated the ink used to write the message was well over two hundred years old.

"Screw this, it'll end up on a display and be overlooked anyway," he said under his breath. Growing slightly more agitated, he slammed his fist against the desktop. "It's not like anybody comes to my blasted museum anymore!"

Gripping both objects loosely in his left hand, he reached into a shelf under his desk with his free hand and took out a circular key chain. He stood up from his leather chair and moved out of his office, pacing through the labyrinth of exhibits that made up the Boston Museum. He stared into the PIRATES AND PRIVATEERS glass display and found an empty space on the shelf full of newspaper clippings, ancient weapons, and old doubloons.

Michael sighed as he inserted the key into the display lock, twisting slowly and opening the glass pane. Directly in front of him was a book on Sir Francis Drake's circumnavigation of the world and a few motley artifacts from other privateer's numerous excursions. He placed the cursed staff and the message on an empty shelf space, and closed the display, locking the window with yet another disappointed sigh.

He stood there until a beeping sound from above brought him to his senses. He craned his neck and saw the red blinking surveillance camera light, its lens pointing out at the empty hall. As he turned away, a faint light encircled the magical staff and an orange and yellow haze rose slowly and eerily, to highlight an article headlined JUNE 26, 1763, CONSPIRACY IN THE KING'S COURT.

3

1595
London, England

The queen of England stared deeply into the eyes of her visitor. Elizabeth smiled; it had been many years since Sir Francis Drake had last stood before her. She broke her stare and looked at the metals and ribbon pinned on nearly every available stitch of his uniform.

"Be seated, my dear Francis. Time has treated you well, as I would have expected it to. I am glad to hear of the success of your recent voyage."

"Thank you, my queen." He bowed. "We leaked our position logs and reports as instructed. The Piri Re'is map was quite detailed and exceedingly accurate, aiding in our circumnavigation around the globe, but Atlantis was nowhere to be found. It is to my belief that no one had any knowledge of our true intentions, or even what we were doing, so I believe we can successfully continue the search at a later time."

"Yes, yes, perhaps Atlantis was a rumor all along, then." The queen paused, collecting her thoughts. "Then again, maybe it is not. But for now, we must focus on other things. I require you to attack the fortress of *El Morro* in San Juan. Our intelligence speculates that it is heavily fortified. We are drawn to the Spanish Main by its firm grasp on New World silver. King Phillip must have a stockpile somewhere between Europe and the colonies, most likely at *El Morro*, where he stores the precious items and then transports the goods to his treasuries in Spain. If we can control Spanish trade and transport, we can control Spain itself."

Sir Francis Drake ran a hand through his hair, putting thought into the queen's request.

"So, I am to attack *El Morro*?" He waited for her nod before he continued. "That should not be a problem; I have successfully laid siege to many of Phillip's ships and harbors over the years. What is one more?"

The two laughed together for a moment. Once the laughter subsided, she continued. "And that is why you are the right man for the endeavor. It is of great importance to discover what secrets are hidden in the depths of *El Morro*."

"Yes, my queen. I shall ready my men and leave with the utmost haste."

✹✹✹✹

Sir Francis Drake looked through his scope, barely seeing past the lantern that hung at the farthest reach of the vessel. The flame danced inside the lantern on the bowsprit, giving off the faintest light through the dense fog. He hurried below to relay the plan of attack to his gun crews.

A message from the lookout in the foremast crow's nest was passed to the master of the vessel. The faint outline of each *garita* came into view as Drake pressed the scope to his eyes yet again, following the recent report. He pictured each sentry box full of Spanish soldiers, awaiting orders to shoot at his flagship, but he smiled, knowing that his men below were one step ahead and were just about to unleash havoc.

A series of timely explosions lit the dark expanse off the starboard side, illuminating an area large enough to allow him a better view of the complex structure of the fortress. The decks below shook violently as the heavy guns shot explosive rounds toward the thick walls of *El Morro*. The smoke and light from each barrel receded in intensity, causing the night to close around them once again, engulfing the ship in a blanket of darkness.

Cannons hidden high in the crevices of the fortress answered, sending a parade of explosive ordnance arcing overhead. The streaks of fire slashed through the night, making their way to the vessel below. Drake stood beside the steering stand and called out a sequence of orders while the helmsman struggled with the wheel. The depth below the keel dwindled as his flagship proceeded toward the beach that lay at the eastern foot of the fortress.

A moment later, the gun decks below erupted again with a furious roar, bringing down the roofs of several small villas within the protection of the walls. His vessel remained on the tack, and its starboard guns raked the fortress as each barrel was swabbed out and reloaded. The protectors of *El Morro* continued their defense, unleashing their abundant armament at the lone attacking ship.

Drake failed to pay attention to the depths of the surrounding waters, and it wasn't until a loud tearing sound from below shook him from his fixation on gold and glory that he realized he had made a terrible seafaring error. The dueling cannons continued their melodic tunes as he made his way below out of harm's way. Running down the companionway ladder, he reached the fast-flooding compartment in the bilge. Soaked to the knees, he rushed back to order his men to abandon the attack. The portside longboats were lowered to the churning waters below as the vessel came to a halt atop a rocky shoal.

✖✖✖

"Three cheers for the successful defense of *El Morro*!"

The men inside the fortress played a tune of celebration as Drake directed his men out of cannon range in their escape of the sinking ship.

The following morning, the men of *El Morro* discovered a vast treasure lying hidden in the depths of the English flagship. They moved the collection of gold and silver to their own storage rooms inside the protection of the fortress. Inside a chest lay a lone three-foot golden staff topped by a precious garnet stone sparkling with life, hiding a secret of unimaginable worth.

4

June 8, 1763
Somewhere in the Atlantic Ocean

Captain Arthur F. Nelson sat at his desk in his quarters aboard the HMS *Defence*, flipping through the logbooks of the previous journey. He skimmed through his recollections of their recent endeavors: the travel to Grand Bahama to see if Ben's young love, Leah, was still there, the satisfaction of watching the captured Blood Bones and his crew be hanged in a crammed court-yard, and their disastrous shipwreck on the uncharted island. He cracked his back against the chair, stretched his arms skyward, and then returned his gaze to his desk.

He stood up from the chair, pushing it back softly. Nelson paced toward the bookshelf with the logbook in hand. Sifting through several other leather-bound volumes, he replaced the book in the desig-nated spot, and then gripped the soft cover of a crimson journal that belonged to Blood Bones. He was eager to get inside of the mind of its author, a man he'd been paid handsomely to capture. His fingers traced the gold buckle that bound the secrets of its writer inside.

After taking a seat, he slipped off his boots with a push of his toe. Once his feet were free, he shifted his body weight and settled into the curves of the chair. His fingers struggled with the journal's buckle as if the book had a mind of its own, unwilling to give in to a new owner. But after several moments, it finally gave way and opened to a page marked with a feather. He noticed the date and then flipped back toward the first page.

August 7, 1751

This is my first entry since having escaped from the dungeons of El Morro, on the island of San Juan, Puerto Rico. My story begins exactly one year, two hundred and five days ago…

It was a beautiful day, February 18, 1750, when I rode my horse into the stable. After giving the stable boy a coin to house the horse for the night, I hurriedly paced toward the personal quarters of my commanding officer. I was just three months into my sixteenth year, fairly new to the Spanish navy. As one of the most reputable messengers in my unit, I would often carry important documents across all of Spain, from port to port, or garrison-to-garrison. This last message sealed my fate, thereby ending my career just as quickly as it had begun. I had arrived a day earlier than expected due to my keen knowledge of the roads and pathways, and when I approached my commanding officer's door, I found that it was left partially open.

It was as if I was fated to witness the event that followed.

As I reached my hand out to knock on the door, the sound of numerous voices from within made me suddenly pause standing just inches from the small gap. I pressed my ear as closely as I dared, hearing just a few phrases that stood out among the gabble of a heated discussion: "Slaves … El Morro … Drake's Treasure … tomorrow on the ebb tide."

I pieced each phrase as I continued listening, waiting for the scandalous plan to unfold at my very feet. It took a few long moments to clearly understand that my commanding officer wished to leave for El Morro on the morrow's ebb, transporting a vast amount of slaves, and then steal the fortress's holdings, which included the vast treasure of Sir Francis Drake. I asked myself what if I could be appointed charge of such a daring mission? The youthful frenzy in my mind wandered.

My excitement and anticipation edged me ever closer to the doorway's gap. Without realizing it, I brushed my shoulder against the door, and it swung open just a few inches. It was enough, however, to catch the conspirators' attention. I heard half a dozen men inside the chamber as they shifted their weight in the leather chairs to find the cause of their disturbance. The sound forever reverberates in my memories. Twelve eyes stared at me, sending a chill down the length of my spine.

I knew not what to say. A feeble sentence managed to roll off my tongue. "Sir, the message has safely been delivered. I placed the letter directly in his hands."

If they thought I had overheard everything, they neither said nor acted upon it.

"Ah, you are early. I had not expected you for another day. All the better, for I have a daring feat which you faithfully deserve to partake."

I blushed at the compliment, letting a few strategically phrased words blind me from the fact that my superior had indeed knew I bore witness to everything.

"Yes, Hernando, you shall be promoted." My commanding officer crossed the room, standing before me with an extended hand. The scarlet stone on his finger sparkled brightly, catching my eye. "I wish that you join these five men on tomorrow's ebb," he paused, hesitating with the phrase that would follow, "and oversee the treatment of the slaves aboard."

"Aye, sir." An elevated mission would mean more adventure, more thrills, and of course, more gold in my

purse. "I shall be down at the pier before sunup, ready for what looms ahead."

But I was not ready for what loomed ahead, not in the least sense of the phrase. I had been under the impression that I would head a convoy of ships, but oh, was I wrong. We sailed for San Juan with over a thousand slaves between five ships, and I was shackled amongst them. I shall choose to limit my description of our treatment aboard during the month-long transit.

I recall being fed perhaps ten of those days, and the food with which we were provided had been the leftovers of the Spanish crew and officers. And to surmise that the food had any benefit to my health would be a severe overstatement. Handfuls of worms could have been extracted prior to eating, but I'd eat them anyway. I didn't want to, but I willed it. I wanted to survive. I needed all the energy I could muster if there was even the remotest chance of escape. By the end of that trip, of living in a packed environment, among many who were seasick from the crossing, I found myself near skeletal. I remember how my bones nearly protruded through my skin and how weak I was that first time my feet once again touched solid land.

Once we arrived, all the slaves were examined to determine their value as well as their fates. Unlike them, my fate had already been chosen, and I was sent to the dungeons of El Morro. There was one lone window in the dark cell on what I later learned to be the west side of my quarters. I would find count sunsets to pass the days.

The thought of escape came every passing minute. Though I'm not positive of the precise thickness of the stone walls that separated me from freedom, I'm most certain they were many yards thick, too much to dig through.

At the conclusion of each day, I'd mark my stay into the cobblestone that lay beneath my feet. After the first week, I can truly say I'd never missed home so much, not even during the crossing in the bowels of the ship. The captain had had somewhat of a soul, for he let us out to breathe fresh air somewhat regularly. Though it wasn't much, the sea air refreshed our bodies and kindred souls despite the horrid living conditions.

There was a time when I began to count individual seconds, which quickly turned into minutes, and then turned to hours. In my head and on the stone floor, I counted days, weeks, and months. I went mad.

The first three months were uneventful, without interaction with fellow inmates, or even the ill-tempered guardsmen. At every meal, I'd try and strike up a conversation with the man who brought my food to me on circular wooden plates. He'd always shrug me off, ignoring my existence. After another few months, I gave up trying to talk to anyone else. That's when I began talking to myself.

Several months further into my captivity I heard something sweet to my ears. It was the sound of the man in the next cell, given a full day to walk around the perimeter of the fortress. I sat with my ear beside the air holes in the door hoping to hear the conversation.

"So, it's been another six months," a voice said.

"Aye, it has," another replied, most likely a prisoner like myself.

I paced around my dwelling, pondering these words. I knew that my time would be coming soon, and I awaited that temporary freedom anxiously. The thought of being able to roam the grounds at my will gave me hope.

I had waited and waited because there wasn't much else to do. Finally, one day I heard a jingling of keys outside the door instead of the usual creak of a hatch that opened, allowing for my food to be sent in and human wastes to be taken out.

A man dressed in a gray robe emerged into the meager light and introduced himself as Father Saladino. My eyes *first caught gaze of the large gold cross that hung around his neck. Being the religious man that I am, or rather, was, I should have noticed that he did not wear the typical wooden cross that I was so accustomed to seeing on priests. This should have warned me that something was not right, but for the moment I was temporarily overcome with the excitement at the simple thought I'd be free of this cell, even for such a miniscule amount of time.*

He escorted me through a maze of tunnels, dungeons, and barracks that made up the fortress, around several outposts, and up and down several ramps. Finally we arrived at a clearing. I knelt down and ran my hand over a patch of grass that stuck out from a relatively dry splotch of land. I admit it was a relief to feel something other than cobblestone under my bare feet. I can still remember the feeling of the sun beating down on my bare chest as if I was penning this entry outside.

The breeches that hung around my waist were slightly torn, as were the leggings that remained of my once Spanish uniform, a uniform, which I had once taken great pride in wearing. I also had a necklace that my mother had long ago given me hung loosely around my neck. That was all I could call my own. My world possessions were summed up in those two items.

Nelson inched forward on his seat, quick to adjust for comfort as the story of the exciting transition of Hernando Audaz transforming into Captain Blood Bones, began to unravel. He looked at the clock on the shelf to gauge the time left to him before his next round on deck. "Ah, lovely, a whole hour."

✖✖✖

Benjamin Manry walked through the quarters of the ordinaries and the marines on his way to the mess hall. The sailors stood up and touched their brims as their first officer passed by. Once inside, the aroma of fish chowder tickled his nose and teased his growling stomach. He sat down beside Harris and Charles Marconi.

"How are you both doing?" Ben smiled, and looked around the mess hall.

Harris looked at his brother and shook his head. "You know the routine; same old stuff, just a different day. I'm overseeing some work on deck. I'm really looking forward to some time off and exploring England."

Marconi smiled. "Yes, it's been a while since I've been there myself. I know we have some duty to tend to first and foremost, but I'm certain that once our task is complete, we can go our own separate ways for a little while. I'd like to return home for a little while if I can manage."

"What port are we tying up at?" Ben managed to say through bites of dipped bread.

"London. I'd have to take a small vessel or maybe ride up along the Thames to my home in Reading. I live about a day's ride farther if I don't stop anywhere along the way," Charles added.

Ben smiled. "I bet you're excited. When was the last time you've been home?"

His fingers began to count the months and years. "Nearing two years now."

Harris sighed. "Whoa, you should throw a party!"

The group laughed. "Well, I wouldn't be surprised if there's a banquet held once we arrive, it is almost the summer solstice, after all. I heard a rumor that news of our last mission was dispatched to England prior to our departure. We might have to make an appearance before King George III and the royal family."

"Wow!" He had learned a little about the reign of King George III and how he had ended up going insane. He kept that information to himself. "That would be excellent. Have you ever been to a king's banquet?"

There was a pause. "Once, many years ago, but I'll tell you about it after watch."

The brothers nodded with enthusiasm. "That'd be great!"

When Ben heard stories in the first person rather than reading about the tales in textbooks, it was as if their history classes came alive.

"Aye, I must depart for now. I've some business to attend." They passed their bowls to the waiting hands of a galley steward before the group of officers walked through the amidships companionway to carry on their duties.

✳✳✳✳

*N*elson looked from the clock back to the alluring crimson journal, eager to learn more about Blood Bones. He continued with the August 7, 1751 entry.

> *I stretched my legs out, walking throughout the boxed courtyard. The fresh air seemed to cleanse my soul and mind, almost making up for the past six months lost in the darkness of my cell. It had now been seven months into my captivity, the first month of which we transited the Atlantic.*
>
> *No single word can describe how I felt that day, but the events that soon transpired could be tagged with the terms, "deceit" and "ill-fate". Father Saladino walked several paces behind me, and it is likely that he noticed that the length of my stride had changed.*
>
> *Once we were shoulder to shoulder, I said to the man, "Father, do you know why I was sentenced here?"*
>
> *He studied my young face, "You are probably like every other one of you here, common street criminals and rebels."*
>
> *I stared into his cold green eyes, seeing through his lie. "But Father, I have done nothing wrong. I just don't understand."*
>
> *He ignored me, staring off at the crashing waves of*

the Atlantic and San Juan Bay. He closed his eyes as he recalled a discussion he had with someone many months ago and he realized that I was truly not there for any petty crime. "Well, it is time to return back."

I suppose I should have been grateful for the time I had been given, but it was not enough.

"Everyone else got a full day to walk these ramparts! Why do I only get an hour?"

Father Saladino called for a guard to come over. "Get Carlos. We have trouble."

Carlos, I later found out, was the head of the dungeons and in charge of the inmates as well as overseeing all aspects of the place. I learned of his name at the conclusion of the whippings I received upon the return to my cell. The man trailed off as he turned on a heel, "Remember my name, Carlos Santiago."

Over the next six months, I dwelled upon his words over and over again. There were then over three hundred and sixty scratch marks in the stones that lined the flooring, and I was determined to do something about my captivity. I had to; I did not want to die inside these stonewalls.

Eventually, the door to my cell opened once again. Father Saladino entered with a smile on his face. "Well, it has been another six months." He glanced at me with evil green eyes.

I could only muster a slight nod; my throat was parched due to the cutback of my water rations. I can only assume I had said something that wasn't appreciated by someone. Saladino led me out of my cell, once again through the maze of tunnels, dungeons, and barracks that made up the fortress, around outposts, and up and down the ramps. Once again, I saw the same patch of grass, though this time it was long dead, whether by drought or the season.

This was the second time we talked. Again, Father Saladino did not say much, nor did he answer any of my questions. But I knew he knew why I was there, and I wanted to hear it for myself. His stubbornness didn't surprise me; it was what happened next that turned my world inside out.

I asked him something he had been asked countless times before. "Can you help me, Father Saladino?"

He shook his head. "Only God can help you, my son."

I reached to my neck, showing him the handcrafted silver chain that still dangled around my neck. I remember his smile the moment I said, "What if I give you this? It's pure silver. My mother was a jeweler and made this especially for me. It's the only thing I have left to my name of value."

He placed his greedy fingers around the medallion, weighing it in his hands. "God can help you, just as I also."

I tried to hide a smile. I should have known better...

The next six months passed by in the same mind wrecking way. The familiar sound of a key on a key ring awakened me from a slight nap. I followed the black-robed thief, Father Saladino silently. No words passed between us until we were finally outside, and when we were, the bright and sunny sky went immediately gray. The sun hid behind the clouds, causing the courtyard to darken. I would swear that the second it happened, I heard him sigh with relief, as if he had deliberately told the sky to change to set up the next scene in his favor.

I noticed now that not only did he have that ugly gold cross around his neck, but now he also wore my mother's keepsake as well. The sight made me angry, causing instant hatred inside myself boil upwards since he had not yet followed through with his promise to help me.

"When is God going to get me out of here?"

He looked at the sky. "When the sun shows once again, that is when you shall make your escape." He paused to build suspense. Pointing to a far off outpost, he continued, "Go there. Inside you will find all that you'll need."

My gaze was fixed on the sky. We spent perhaps an hour just looking upwards at the thick clouds. When the sun finally did shine through I made my dash for freedom.

"Guards! That prisoner is trying to get away!"

Those words echoed across the courtyard, cried out by the black-robed thief, Father Saladino. From the corner of my eye, I saw a man kneel down, his rifle pointed just ahead of me. I knew that if I continued running, my life would end, so I dove to the ground just as I heard the click of the trigger being pulled and the round explode from the barrel. The man to whom I had entrusted my only treasure had betrayed me.

I stood up as fast as I could and continued my sprint, glancing over my shoulder every few feet. The guard was readying his rifle for another volley. I gauged the distance that remained and increased my gait.

I reached the edge of the courtyard. I breathed a sigh of relief as I made my way up an angled staircase just as another shot rang out. This time the aim was for my lower back, and just as I paced up the next flight of stairs I heard a loud thud. The ball ricocheted off the stone staircase, showering my feet with debris. I stumbled forward, crashing hard into the corner of the next landing. I just had to round the corner and I would temporarily be out of harm's way. I glanced over my shoulder as I pushed my weight and stood straight.

As I continued to the second floor of the outpost, I sensed trouble and decided to round the corner with a lowered shoulder. I smelled the alcohol on the man's breath before I even saw him. He had his pistol aimed toward my chest as I barreled into him. His finger slipped and pulled the trigger just as I stumbled over his lower half. Our two bodies fell to the floor in a mix of punches and kicks. Being quick and nimble I got to my feet first as the man struggled in his intoxicated state to recover from my blows. I quickly considered my options, and came to the abrupt conclusion that I had none left. Not only did a rifleman close off my escape in the courtyard, but also now I heard several voices from above.

I angled my body and stepped back into the shadows, hoping I was invisible to the courtyard. From my new perspective, I realized I was just several feet from a rampart that may perhaps lead to my salvation. Swiftly, I took the small gap in one leap, exposing myself just for a brief moment to the rifleman in the courtyard, and scurried over the rampart wall. There I discovered a small gully that linked up with a higher rampart. I turned my head and heard the quickened footsteps of my pursuers. I did not wait to see whom they belonged to.

My arms stretched upward, reaching for the eight-foot high wall. I knew I would have to jump. As my body sprung upwards, my hands soared high and I felt the jar on my body as I gripped the top of the wall. I pulled myself up and just as I had swung my left leg over, the rifleman emerged into view. I saw him raise his weapon, aimed at me.

There was not much else that I could do and I closed my eyes and said a quick prayer, hoping to survive. The skies had opened up earlier, and now the sun brightened its magnitude to an almost blinding intensity. Blinded by the glare the rifleman had difficulty placing his sights on me, and I fully cleared the top of the wall. Without looking, my momentum carried my body over.

For the next one hundred feet, my body tumbled down to the warm waters of San Juan Bay. To say I was not afraid would be a lie, but it felt as though all my *problems had just ended then and there. I formed an arrow before my body entered the water. But as if God was truly looking after me, my body sank deep into the water and then popped back up like a cork, without any injuries. I looked up at the great distance, seeing the corroded rocks that lined El Morro's edges. I did not know what to do then, or where to go. I let the current chose my fate to deliver me to where I was destined to be.*

✖✖✖

The western sky danced brilliantly with a hue of red and orange, giving way for the rising stars to the east. Ben paced the decks, hearing the bell toll the time. Watching a pod of dolphins play off the bow, Ben heard the slow traipse of footsteps behind him, giving warning of someone approaching. He smiled as Charles came to stand at the rail beside him.

"Good evening, Ben. How's the watch going?" Charles smiled in greeting.

Ben laid an elbow atop the rail and looked off at the great blue beyond. "Just enjoying the last few moments of light. Waiting for the stars to come out. Other than that, we have a strong, following wind. At mid-watch we were making a little more than ten knots."

Marconi did a quick calculation in his head, noting his vessel's progress. "Aye, that's good news, then. I suppose in less than two weeks' time we'll be in sight of England."

Ben nodded. "Yes, sir, as long as the wind remains constant." He paused for a minute, enjoying the fresh breeze on his face. "This is my first trans-Atlantic crossing, and I hope there are many others after this. It's such an adrenaline rush you know? It's us versus the sea. It's the ultimate adventure!"

Marconi let out a booming laugh that carried with the wind. "You've got many seas to travel, my young friend and many adventures loom before you. But until then, I shall tell you a tale of my younger years. Perhaps you may learn a thing or two from it."

Ben prompted the story with an excited nod and turned his attention from the flat horizon surrounding him to Charles.

"Well, before I describe my first banquet, I should probably tell you of the two battles that afforded me the opportunity to attend the event." Charles cleared his throat, preparing the way for his tale. "It began when I was about your age. I signed aboard with James Cook as a cabin boy on the collier brig *Friendship*. If memory serves me correct he was a mate then, and I his apprentice. I am sure it sounds a familiar story," he said, knowing that Ben similarly did the same. "In 1755 he entered the Royal Navy as master's mate on the HMS *Eagle*. I continued serving him as he moved up the ranks. Next he sailed as boatswain. In 1756 Cook had a temporary post as the master of the *Cruizer* and then in June 1757 we found ourselves on the frigate HMS *Solebay*, where we encountered several minor skirmishes off the coasts of Britain." Charles paused for a moment, allowing Ben to catch up.

"And did you also get promoted?" Ben asked with an excited smile.

"Aye, but I am getting to that," Charles said, building the suspense of the tale. "So, as I continue with the story, the Seven Years' War began to spiral out of control on several fronts, as I am sure you know from your studies. Captain Cook was given the HMS *Pembroke*, and in 1758 we took part in a large-scaled amphibious assault. We captured the city of Louisbourg from the French. As a result of this, Cook promoted me to third officer, a position with which I was slightly surprised, because I didn't truly do that much in the battle. However, he said it was a reward for my loyal service over the years. I thanked him and swore an oath to contribute more to my duties. I volunteered to lead a surveying expedition up the Saint Lawrence River during the siege of Quebec City. While doing this, Captain Cook helped me with the mapping procedure. This is where I made a name for myself in our service to King and Country."

Harris paced over to the group to relieve the watch. He greeted Ben and Charles and then began the turnover routine. He scanned the horizon, making sure there were no vessels or land in sight before he surveyed the sheets above, noting the tightness in the sails as the wind continued to push the vessel onward.

"Looks like I have a quiet night ahead of me." Harris put a hand on his younger brother's shoulder.

"Hey buddy, yeah, it was pretty quiet. I put a fix on the chart at the beginning of watch; we made some decent progress, averaged about ten knots since the morning. Latest estimate for arrival in London is thirteen days. We are on our intended course, so you shouldn't have to adjust the sails unless the wind shifts." Ben began his turnover. "No contacts to be passed on. Deck work ended at sunset. Wind has been steady off the port quarter, blowing at about twenty knots. Current is setting us a bit to starboard. We had to tend the sails earlier to get a bit more out of them. Good visibility, you should be able to do a latitude by Polaris and the moon rises in an hour."

Harris smiled. "Great, sounds good. Full moon?"

Ben nodded. "Yeah. Close to it, at least. I think it'll be full tomorrow, but you should still be able to see the horizon pretty clearly."

"Okay, I got the watch," Harris said. "So, what are you guys up to?"

"Charles was telling me that story he mentioned at lunch," Ben replied.

Marconi nodded. "Harris, attend to your business; make sure your men know what to expect for the watch and then return back here for the rest of the tale. I stopped just as we were about to lay siege to Quebec."

"Oh, giving the Canadians the boot, eh?" Harris laughed.

Ben and Charles smiled as Harris tended his duties while the two enjoyed a few moments of shared silence. Their eyes stared off into the crashing waves, following the speckles of foam being tossed around gently by the wind.

Harris returned after a few moments and Charles cleared his throat. "So, to catch you up with the my youthful endeavors, if you picture the two of your stories of advancing up the ranks, mine is quite similar. I was cabin boy and apprentice to James Cook. After several small battles on the eve of the Seven Years' War, I was promoted to third officer. We surveyed the St. Lawrence River, and were supposed to meet two other ships to converge on Quebec. Unfortunately, of the three, we were the only crew to make it there at the designated rendezvous. We were severely outnumbered. Supposedly information of our attack fell into Montcalm's hands. He was the French general of the garrison. We were pretty much at a stalemate for the first few days. General Wolfe got sick, and in his delusions and nightmares, thought it a good idea to attack, so beginning the night of September 12, 1759 and on until the next morning, we managed to cross the river and moved over four thousand troops and guns up the towering protective cliffs, called the Heights of Abraham. The Frenchies didn't expect that many of our troops at the unprotected location and there we moved forward, achieving an easy victory."

Ben smiled. "So that was that then?"

Charles nodded. "Yes, for the most part at least. We fought for a few days more and Quebec surrendered on the eighteenth, ending their chances of maintaining their dominance in the New World. Both generals succumbed to fatal wounds, but Wolfe lived to see the victory."

"That was a great story," Harris said. "So then you went to the king's banquet?"

Before Marconi could respond, Ben chimed in, "I thought you said there were two battles."

"Aye, there were two. That was just the first, which as I said essentially ended the dominance of the French in America. But our next battle had an even more important outcome."

Marconi cleared his throat again, and then continued the tale.

"King George II passed word to all available ships to make haste back to London. Our intelligence informed us that the French intended to invade England and Scotland. Just a few months before, at the Battle of Lagos, we'd sunk two French ships of the line and captured three, which had removed the threat in the Mediterranean Sea. Onward we went, under the leadership of Admiral Hawke. We had a blockade set against the French off the coast of Brest. A westerly gale blew in and forced the majority of our ships to seek shelter at Torbay on the south coast of England, but we had left a few ships to keep an eye on the French at Quiberon Bay. There was a steady wind for the most part of a week, but then it shifted easterly, and under cover of night Commander Conflans led the French out of the blockade."

"Those sneaky Frenchies!" Harris smiled.

The group chuckled and then Charles continued with his story.

"Our fleet was split, and Conflans moved in for the easy victory. He probably would've succeeded, too, had the wind not shifted in our favor. Hawke's remaining ships sailed hard, putting out every sheet to the wind. We lost two ships to those blasted shoals, but we sunk six of theirs and captured one." Charles paused to take a breath, whispering a silent prayer for his lost comrades. He stared off into the darkness before continuing. "The battle could have gone either way under calm seas, each side having roughly the same number of over twenty ships. But the wind kept shifting and a gale was blowing mighty hard, putting us at the advantage for the time being. The French lost many ships and many good sailors; we won a decisive battle that essentially eliminated the French navy from the rest of the war."

"Whoa! So those were the two key battles you fought in then?" Ben asked. "I'm guessing you were then invited to the king's banquet as a result?"

"Yes, yes. The events coincided with the celebration for the Vernal Equinox in 1760. I was one among many of the brave sailors and marines who fought in the battles that crippled our French enemies. There were many of our British army friends and comrades in attendance at the event as well. I met Sir Robert Clive, Baron of Plassey, as well as several of his very loyal officers who'd fought bravely in the India campaign. Then there were many other officers who'd fought on the European fronts of that long and battle-ridden war. Overall it was a great event, with much laughter, good food, and even more important, fine delicacies and rare wines. It was the king's last banquet, however. He passed away a few months later on an early morning at the end of October. His grandson, George III, took his place."

5

June 15, 1763
Brighton, England

Captain Richard Highmore, thirty-two years of age, was a member of the Fourteenth Regiment stationed in Bombay, India during Britain's struggle with Holland, Spain, and France throughout the Seven Years' War. There, Britain protected and expanded her trading rights and territorial gains.

After his marriage to the beautiful Leah Williamson, a young damsel of eighteen years originating from Grand Bahama, the couple settled on a large four hundred acre estate in Brighton, located in South Downs. His family was worth well over £5 million and his property suitably displayed his wealth. Fountains lined the road that led to the estate, which zigzagged around the small plantations that were located on the Highmore grounds. With access to the sea on the southernmost area of his property, he had several personal yachts, which he often enjoyed on a nice summer day.

Leah sat quietly in her room, combing her long hair after a hot bath. Sitting wrapped in a bath sheet, she stared around the room with her mouth open. She was not used to such luxury. Although being the daughter of a governor had allowed her an above-average lifestyle, this new level was near regal.

As she replaced Ben's medallion around her neck, she noticed the sunlight filtering through the open window. The evening's last rays danced upon the golden treasure that hung on her bosom. She smiled, holding onto the thoughts of the young man who had captured her heart. There was a knock on the door and then the familiar face of Eve, a fourteen-year-old Negro slave who had been born on the estate, emerged into view.

"Hello, Eve. How are you?"

The girl curtseyed. "I am well. May I help with your hair?"

Leah glanced into the mirror, seeing the tangled mess. With a smile she said, "Yes, that would be nice."

"Dinner will be ready in half an hour, my lady." Eve smiled as she entered the room and positioned herself next to Leah. She handed Eve the ivory inlaid comb, and then relaxed into the curves of the carved wooden chair. Eve stood behind Leah and began to untangle the strands of her mistress's golden locks with her left hand, while running the comb through with her right.

"Your hair is so beautiful."

Leah's cheeks turned red with the compliment. "Thank you, darling. I love how you do your hair. I would like it if you could perhaps you can do mine like yours one day, when my husband is away of course. I know he would not approve, nor think well of it."

The girls snickered together.

❈❈❈

Twenty minutes passed as Eve helped Leah with her outer garments. Slipping her shoes on, Leah walked gracefully with Eve down the staircase to the dining hall. The countless platters of food billowed steam as the servers opened their covers.

Richard Highmore already sat at the table, reading a letter he had opened. His gaze shifted to his wife once Eve had pulled Leah's chair back for her.

"Hello, dear."

Leah curtsied, and while still unaccustomed to her new marriage, she smiled awkwardly. She replied quietly, "How was your day?"

He had arrived just an hour before. "Uneventful my dear. Just the usual business; meetings and training the new recruits for army life."

She looked at the letter in his hand. "Dear, what's that?"

Before answering, he read it over again. "Just an invitation to a banquet in London, hosted by King George III on the twenty-second."

She smiled. "Oh, I shall look forward to it! Who is the distinguished guest, or are there several?" She remembered the last time she had dressed up for such an honored event. "I only have a week to find a suitable dress!"

He smiled at his wife's concern, running a hand over his fire-red hair. It was tied back into a tightly greased ponytail. The light from the candles above glimmered off his locks.

He glanced at the letter in his hand. "It mentions several names: Captain Nelson of the HMS *Defence,* and his three officers, Charles Marconi, Nate Brodkin, and Benjamin Manry," He picked up speed toward the end of the list. "A week is plenty of time, I think I will attend the event in uniform."

The names had been read too quickly for her to make any connection. She replied, "Well, that's just too easy! That really takes the fun and excitement out of it all. What am I going to wear then?"

"I'll take a trip tomorrow and find you something suitable for a woman of such beauty."

She blushed at the compliment, releasing a forced and unnatural giggle. "Thank you, perhaps something to match my eyes? An offset blue-green?"

They said grace and began eating the meal set before them. The only sounds heard in the dining room were the chewing of food and the scraping of forks and knives against their plates as they cut through the curried venison and various other delicacies. There was quiet that lingered over the table as she stared off into space; on the wall to her left her imagination suddenly formed a face. The longer she stared, the more clearly Ben's features began to take form. She suddenly realized one of the distinguished guests her husband had mentioned would be Ben, a man who she had fallen in love with as quickly as he had come into her life. The fact that she would see him again nearly knocked her off her chair.

"Is everything all right, Leah?"

"Oh, yes. Everything's fine," she replied, but her awkwardness lasted well until after dessert ended. Soon the servants came into the room to retrieve the place settings. He stood up and moved to where Leah was standing. He helped pull out the chair and offered his hand to help her up. Though he was a gentleman, she simply had no authentic feelings for him, nothing even remotely comparable to what she still felt for Ben.

"Thank you. I am not feeling well. I could use some fresh air."

✖✖✖

As Leah walked along the cobblestone walkway, Ben's face began to take form on inanimate things: a tree, a reflection, a cloud. Even after shaking her head to get his deep, blue eyes and thick, dark hair out of her mind, his image took form once more, this time in a bush that bordered a grand fountain. As she kneeled by the fountain, tears began to flow down the curves of her cheek. She looked into the water that sat under four tiers of the fountain, noticing the ripples as her tears fell in the water below, and then dispersed with the fountain water. Once the surface was calm again, there were now two faces staring back at her. She wept until the images of her and Ben faded through sheets of tears, hoping secretly their paths would cross again.

6

June 18, 1763
At Sea

Ben entered his cabin holding a sextant case firmly in his hand. He had a piece of paper sandwiched between his fingers and the wooden case that contained the time of his observation of the sun scribbled down neatly. He sat at the desk and went to work on the reduction of local apparent noon. Opening and closing various nautical publications and almanacs, he plotted a line of latitude and labeled it with a time and date. He then opened a logbook, which contained the average speed for the day, and after a quick calculation, advanced a morning line of position to intersect at 1200. Content with his position, he measured off the distance from the volcanic archipelago of the Azores to his plotted position. He then entered the coordinates into the Official Deck Logbook.

He took a parallel ruler and measured the angle from the position he had just plotted to England. He drew a light line and carefully measured the distance that remained for the journey. His fingers traced each noon fix for the journey since Boston. They grew ever closer to their destination, and he smiled, eagerly awaiting the next mission and the adventures that loomed ahead.

✷✷✷

The evening sun was slowly descending as Captain Nelson inspected the decks on a round of his vessel. Men worked over the side doing general maintenance. A few sailors were painting on the port side to ready the vessel for its stay in London. He smiled as he watched several younger cabin boys shine the brass bell that tolled the time every half hour. Pleased that all was ship-shape, he walked leisurely to his cabin.

Once inside the comfort of his stateroom, he sat before the crimson journal that lay open on his desk, eager to read more of the thoughts and adventures of the infamous pirate. He was completely absorbed by the intoxicating words of Blood Bones, and he felt as if he was a part of the story. He flipped to the next page, looking at the date.

August 8, 1751

The current was strong as it dragged my body between the sharp rocks along the coastline. About a mile from where I landed, there was a small shipyard. I climbed up the wharf and crept between mounds of driftwood for cover. There were several vessels at anchor or in dry dock. I could feel the sun on my back, drying my waterlogged body. The breeches that hung on my waist provided very little protection from the sun. I crept past a series of woodshops where men hammered at the hull of a new fishing vessel. One man used a plane to shave off sections to curve the keel. On my haunches, I continued my trek to find a main street and a way back to civilization.

The sunburn on my back irritated the scars of my whippings, slowing me to a feeble trot. I crept into an alleyway and hid beneath a disheveled tarp of shredded cloth that looked to be centuries old. I wrapped this around my bare upper body and slept for many hours.

It must have been the middle of the night when I left

my hiding place in search of food. My hair was down to my shoulders. I knew that I smelt, but my nose was so used to the stench of El Morro. I had no money to my name; the only thing I had had of value now clung to the neck of Father Saladino. It angered me knowing me that he had robbed me of my sole possession. I then swore an oath, eager to begin my revenge upon those who had betrayed me.

    I remember the wind that blew on that street, pushing me towards my destiny. I found myself opening a tavern door. Once I stepped inside, I noticed several eyes turn toward me, but as I closed the door, their gazes focused back to the bottoms of their mugs. I made my way around tables and approached the bar.

    I did not know what to say, but I could tell the barkeep knew I needed something. "Sir, I do not have money, or anything to give you, but I was hoping you could perhaps be able to give me a meal and a place to sleep for the night? I would be happy to work in the kitchen or run errands, or anything you need sir."

    The man's face wrinkled into a frown. "I'm afraid that's not possible." His gaze shifted to the floor, to avoid the appearance of guilt as I began to turn on a heel.

    I called over my shoulder, "Well, have a good night then, sir."

    I do not know exactly why he called back to me as I limped my way to the door, but I can only speculate that he might have seen the crisscrossed pattern of scars on my back in the dim light emanating from the lanterns and candles within the tavern.

    "Wait. Come back," he called out. His voice carried over the boisterous laughter and music that filled the room.

    My eyes stared at the candelabrum that hung above the man's head. Seven candles burned brightly, seven candles that gave me hope.

    "Yes?" was the only word that I could muster.

"*Let me get you a dish from the kitchen. It is only scraps, mind you and I do have a room. It's small, but it'll do for the night,*" *he said through a genuinely friendly smile.*

I knew that for the first time in years, I had a friend.

"*Thank you.*" *I replied with a smile.* "*I greatly appreciate your kindness.*"

I waited by the counter, and minutes later the tavern owner came out with a bowl of thick seafood bisque. On a platter were two hard rolls along with a mug of water. For the first time in a very long time, my stomach was actually full. It was the most memorable meal I have ever eaten. After dining, the owner showed me to my room.

He let me stay for a week. He only asked that I help around the tavern in the kitchen, scrubbing pots and pans and the occasional food run. He even gave me an old shirt and leather moccasins. Each night I would tell him, and whoever else dared to listen, the story of my escape from El Morro. Passersby would sometimes stop and toss me a coin, after hearing of the hardships that I had been through at my young age.

On the last day of my stay, my fate took another twist and turn.

Two men entered the tavern in hopes of recruiting sailors. Our eyes met and they approached.

"*How old are you, lad?*" *one man asked.*

"*I turned eighteen just a month ago, sir.*"

"*What's your name?*"

"*Audaz. Hernando Audaz.*"

My last name seemed to have rung a bell, for I saw a hint of a smile grow. "*Are you of any relation to Álvaro?*"

I speculated that the stranger was a sailor, although that of the "non-merchant" kind, and must have been acquainted with this Álvaro; I sensed an opportunity and quickly told him that he was my cousin.

He studied my physique as we chatted about my family relations. "You're a little on the thin side, eh?"

Though the weeklong stay in the tavern had put some meat on my bones once again, I was still deprived of the healthy form I had once known. "I had a long few years …" I trailed off.

He saw a trail of scars on my left shoulder as I reached to my neck to scratch an itch, my meager clothing shifting slightly. My hair was still a long, tangled mess. "Come with me to the back room. I have some questions for you."

I followed him and his companion into the neighboring room. Once seated, he stared at me. "Tell me of these misfortunes that have clearly befallen you."

I summarized the now familiar story, which left my small audience in awe. "You would perhaps like a chance to avenge yourself with the Spanish?"

I nodded.

"Along with the English, the Dutch, the Portuguese, and whoever else that we decide to run through?" His smile grew ever larger as he listed the countries.

I smiled. I began to consider how I might take my vengeance upon Father Saladino and Captain Bernardo Bermudez for sending me to the depths of Hell. "Yes."

I only needed to say that one word, and as quickly as I had entered that friendly tavern just a week earlier, I exited it in company of the men I would soon forge powerful friendships and partnerships with. Before I was completely out the door, I waved to the tavern owner, and my expression of thanks lingered in the air as I passed through the doorway.

A growl from his stomach caused Nelson to stir. He stretched his neck and then looked at the clock. It was time for a round of the ship and for his evening meal.

7

June 21, 1763
Off the Coast of England

Near one in the morning the two English vessels sailed in convoy, rounding the spit of land that was Dover. Keeping to their starboard edge of the strait, Captain Nelson gave the helmsman a command to alter course for what would soon become the entrance to the River Thames. He looked at the vessel following in his wake. The HMS *Courtesy* was lagging not far behind on the crisp horizon. Through his scope, he saw Marconi and Ben leaning against the bowsprit and he then scanned the shores on either side of his vessel, noting several lights and flickers of fires from the villages that dotted the hills.

✖✖✖

The sun rose slowly. It was the summer solstice, the longest day of the year. Ben was halfway into his watch when the lands on either side began to draw together, forming the mouth of the River Thames. He saw a village, with smoke rising from a cluster of chimneys on the north shore. He moved briskly across deck to Marconi's quarters.

"Southend, abeam to starboard, sir!"

He smiled, looking up from his desk, which was covered with paperwork. "Good, we're almost there. Just less than forty miles left.

By the end of the next watch, we should be on the city borders of London."

Ben nodded toward Marconi. "Aye, I'll stay on deck after I'm relieved. Will you be coming up?"

"Yes." Marconi slurped down the remaining tea and left the empty cup on his desk.

He wiped his lips with a handkerchief and then stood up and joined Ben at the doorway. The steps creaked under their combined weight as they climbed the after companionway to main deck. They moved as far forward as they could, and took a position at the bowsprit, leaning against the forward rail as a slight breeze ruffled their hair. Ben looked down at the displaced water as the bow cut through the water, seeing several fish swimming alongside.

✷✷✷

Eve tightened the white corset, stringing the two lengths of cord between a series of clasps that ran parallel to Leah's spine. Once the corset was tightly in place around her bosom, Leah began pulling on her silk leg stockings, further readying herself for the king's banquet and masquerade.

"Eve, please hand me my petticoat." She pointed to the chair.

"Yes, madam," Eve replied.

As she continued to dress, Eve went to the window to let in fresh air. She paused at the sill and saw the sun inching just above the hillside in the eastern part of the estate. A horse-drawn carriage slowly made its way through the property's winding roads.

Leah then stared into the grand cedar closet that housed all her gowns and dresses. Her eyes remained motionless, staring at the white gown that reminded her of time spent with Ben before he had left on his grand journey.

"I wonder how he's doing." The words escaped in a sigh, as she closed her eyes hoping to erase the thoughts and images that raced through her head.

Eve came to her side, away from assorting the selected jars of perfumes and fragrances with which Leah would adorn for the evening that she was eager to attend, yet equally hesitant.

"Madam, is everything all right?"

Eve was the only member of the household marginally close to her in age. The two would often take long walks around the property, stopping at the fountains to relax and enjoy the scenery.

"Yes, I suppose. I am having second thoughts about attending."

Her personal servant moved closer, placing a comforting hand on her shoulder.

"What's wrong, madam?"

"Do you remember the name Ben, the lad that saved my mother and I from an attack shortly before I came here?"

Eve replied instantly, remembering Leah's detailed description of the young man. "Yes," she said quickly with the building excitement that comes with two young girls talking about a boy, "of course. How could I forget the wonderful stories you told me of him?"

"Well, he's one of the honored guests at the banquet." Leah paused, sniffing back a tear that seemed destined to escape her eye. "I suppose I'm afraid that if I see him, I won't ever get him out of my dreams and thoughts."

"And is that bad?" Eve chuckled.

Leah smiled. "No, of course not, but I'm married."

"Do you even love him?"

She looked at Eve blankly. "Love whom? My husband, or Ben?"

Seeing an opportunity to kill two birds with one stone, Eve replied tactfully. "Both."

"Well, my husband's a good man; a very kind, generous, and respectful gentleman. Any woman would be happy to have him as a husband. He treats me well and he honors my privacy. I suppose that love could grow in time ..." she trailed off, looking down into the folds of her crossed arms, avoiding the question that her lips wanted to say.

"Be that as it may, but that does not answer my question," Eve replied with a smile. "And what of Ben?"

She sighed; a feeling of warmth spread through her body when his name was mentioned. "Yes, I love him. He's everything I want in a man! He is handsome, successful, and just perfect for me in every way! Unlike Richard, who is my senior by many years, Ben is young, we could live a long and healthy life, growing old together."

Knowing that her point was proven, Eve smiled. "Now let's get you dressed all nice and pretty; you've got a man to see!"

Eve reached into the cedar closet to remove the beautiful dress that her master had purchased just days earlier for Leah. It was a silver embroidered, blue damask court Mantua, with an elegantly laced open-fronted gown with an elaborate train.

It was a perfect fit.

❌❌❌

A fleet of small, single-mast fishing boats met the two English flagged vessels. Nelson walked to the railing and peered over the side.

"Greetings!" Nelson removed his cover and waved the tri-corn hat. "How're you?" He hollered down to his fellow countrymen with cupped hands.

The sun had reached its apex as they entered the harbor.

The messenger stared at the name painted on the hull, then called up. "Great! How was the crossing, sir?"

"Not too bad, hit a little rough weather at one point, but other than that, rather uneventful. But I suppose after the last few months, uneventful is a good thing," he chuckled. He did not wait for a response. "Do I have any messages?"

The man looked through a bundle of letters. "Yes." He craned his head upward. "A package from the king, himself."

Nelson concentrated, remembering the day of the month. "Oh, yes, the summer solstice!"

"Aye, tonight is the banquet and masquerade. Here, catch this," he said as he wrapped an envelope stuffed with the invitations into a blanket, and then tied it off tightly with a cord, leaving the end coiled in his right hand.

With a heave, the line soared through the air. Grabbing the end, Nelson pulled up the remaining cord, cradling the blanket-wrapped package to his chest.

"Thanks," he said. He removed a coin from his pocket and dropped it down to the man below. He watched the sun shimmer off the rotating coin as it fell into the eager hands of the fisherman.

Nelson turned and paced toward the after companionway ladder. Once in his quarters, he untied the knot and spread out the blanket to reveal its contents. The invitations were beautifully adorned, hand-written on steam-pressed paper. Sliding a finger under the wax seal, he noticed the king's unique mark and smiled as he began reading the invitation addressed to him.

Captain Arthur F. Nelson,

I request your attendance for the celebration of the summer solstice. I will be hosting a banquet and masquerade at Buckingham Palace, on the evening of the twenty first of June. A carriage will pick up you and your officers at the wharf at five. The event starts at seven o'clock. We will dine in the State Ballroom and after the conclusion of the meal and dance we shall view a light show in the outer courtyard. I also wish to speak with you and your officers on matters concerning your next assignment.

King George III

The only knowledge of the next mission was the name George Grenville, the current Prime Minister of England, on a sheet of paper that also contained the crossed-off names of *El Perro Loco*, Captain Blood Bones, and Blood Spot, among many others from previous missions. He laid the invitation on his desk, wondering what obstacle he and his brave men would be conquering next.

※※※

The officers met on the wharf once both vessels were securely moored and the gangways tended. They discussed the plans for the upcoming evening.

"We've got little more than three hours left before the king's carriage arrives." Nelson coughed and then cleared his throat. "If you'd scrub down of both vessels top to bottom, and then grant liberty to the crew. I would like to host several tours of our ships to the locals if they are interested. Please pass word to the watch standers and have several bulletins made to advertise."

"Yes, sir," replied his officers.

The four men returned to their respective vessels to ready themselves for the upcoming evening.

✖✖✖

Ben stripped out of his clothes, scrubbing away the filth that had accumulated as a result of a hard working life upon the sea. His skin was now red from rubbing, but by the time he'd finished he knew he was clean. He ran his wet hands through his hair, smoothing out the tangles. His bare chest reflected the candlelight as he stared into the small rectangular mirror. Leah's gift hung loosely around his neck. Smiling, he opened the clasp and looked at the small ornate painting.

"I wonder if she's happy, wherever she is," he mumbled.

Ben pulled on fresh undergarments and then dabbed a handful of cologne along the curves of his neck and under his armpits. Slowly, he donned his uniform. There were no medals or ribbons, just some stitching to indicate his rank.

He strung the decorative cutlass on his hip, and then began to pace back and forth before the mirror. He heard a laugh from behind him.

"What are you doing?" Harris mocked.

Ben smiled at his brother. "What does it look like?"

Sal and Jacob joined in. "Getting all dolled up, eh?"

"Oh, shush. You never know if a beautiful princess will be there. Heck, it is a banquet and masquerade hosted by the king, after all," he said with a smile.

"Right, well, you look decent. Just don't forget your shoes."

He looked at his feet. "I guess that'd be a problem," he said as he sat down on his bed.

"You wouldn't want the clock to toll midnight and then be chased by a prince to see if the shoe fit." Sal laughed.

"What a goon, Ben as Cinderella? Ha! What an image," Harris said with a smile, shaking his head.

Ben pulled on his leather uniform boots to his feet, eyeing the shiny brass buckles and soft black leather laces.

"So, what are you guys doing when you get off today?" Ben asked.

"Well, your little get-together is at Buckingham, right?" Harris asked.

Ben nodded as he began lacing the boots.

"Hmm, maybe go to a tavern or something, get some food. When it gets dark we can stand by the front gate and see the fireworks."

Ben looked at his brother. "Sounds good. I talked to Nelson a little while ago. He said that the king wishes to speak with us about our next mission. He mentioned something about Prime Minister George Grenville."

"Hmm, cool, I guess?" Harris said.

"Yeah, we'll see how it pans out." Ben shrugged.

"So, you think she's going to be there?" Harris looked at the opened clasp that hung around Ben's neck.

His face wrinkled. "I hope? I guess? I mean if I see her, I wouldn't even know what to say, or where to begin."

"I know what you mean," Sal chimed in.

Ben shook his head, "Yeah, we never went on that triple date that we promised Molly!"

Harris smiled. "Yeah, you're right. I wonder how she's doing."

Sal sighed. "Well, now that you got me all depressed, let's go to the taverns!"

They laughed as they shook hands, and then he continued readying himself for the evening as the door to his quarters closed, waving one last time as his friends departed. Placing the locket next to his chest, Ben smiled.

"I should really get a haircut soon," he mumbled out loud.

His hair now went well past his eyebrows, and the only feasible way to comb the hair was with a middle part.

🖤🖤🖤

The three officers met Captain Nelson on the wharf at quarter to five; eager for what promised to be a great evening. They reviewed each other's uniforms to pass the time.

"Well, one thing's for certain, we do look outstanding. Now if the carriage would just arrive," Nelson said as he removed his cover, swiping a hand through his hair.

As if on cue, the sound of two horses and the squeaky wheels of a carriage pulled up beside the waiting men, just as a nearby ship's bell tolled the time.

"Good evening. Captain Nelson?" the driver called down from the buggy.

"Yes, that is I. And same to you, thanks for the ride," said Nelson as he motioned for his officers to enter the opened carriage.

Marconi led the way, with Brodkin following and Ben shortly behind. Once all three officers were in, Nelson ducked under and took a seat beside Ben on the red velvet padding.

"Ah, now we just need a bottle of wine and it would be the start to what will be a perfect night!" the captain slapped his thigh with a hearty laugh.

Ben surveyed the interior of the carriage, noticing the craftsmanship in its construction. He smiled as he saw that the neck of a bottle protruded from a cutout section in the corner of the space.

"Who's up for a magic trick?" He paused dramatically once all eyes were on him. "Chilled wine, anyone?" he said, then reached for the bottle and a tray of glasses that had been obscured from view due to a linen cloth covering.

"Oh, Ben, how you surprise us!" Nelson smiled with delight.

"Eh, I try, I try!" The group's laughter echoed through the paths and streets of London as the horses pulled the carriage toward the wondrous spectacle that is Buckingham Palace.

8

June 21, 1763
Buckingham Palace, London

Richard Highmore stood tall, spreading the creases of his uniform coat. He then reached an outstretched hand toward his wife, helping her out of the carriage.

"You look spectacular," he said with a courteous bow as Leah landed lightly beside him.

As she replied, Leah saw Ben's face begin to form upon her husband's shoulders.

"Thanks, you look stunning as well," she said through a forced smile.

He led her to the front gate, where two men stood and asked the couple for their invitation. Reaching inside his breast pocket, Highmore took out the folded envelope.

"Highmore, Captain Richard Highmore," he told the guards as he opened the invitation for them to view. "This is my wife, Leah."

Their gazes were frozen on her beautiful features. One guard sensed the disapproving glare of her husband and broke the silence by clearing his throat. "Ahem, enjoy the festivities. If you will just continue through the gate you can check your seating arrangements."

"Very well, thank you," Richard Highmore said quickly, pulling on Leah's hand.

Leah curtseyed to the event workers as her husband stowed the invitation in his breast pocket and squeezed her hand forcibly. The two walked forward in an awkward silence. Through the front gate and before their eyes emerged a fountain of immaculate beauty. Octagonal in shape, the fountain had an equal amount of differently angled sprays spewing out water in intricate patterns.

"Oh my." She sighed in amazement.

"It's wonderful, but not nearly as breathtaking as our home."

She sensed the pride he had taken in the construction of his, or rather their home. She was still not used to the married life that she had helplessly been thrown into by her father.

"We're an hour early; would you like to go indoors?"

She shook her head. "No, I think I would like to walk around the palace grounds, or just to sit by the fountain for the time being."

✖.✖.✖

*B*en peered out the small carriage-door window, taking in the scenery. He could feel the horses slowing as the carriage came to a gradual stop. The handle turned and the driver's face emerged into view.

"Gentlemen, may I present Buckingham Palace," he said with a bow, pointing an outstretched arm toward the front gate.

He led the group forward and the four naval officers followed.

"Enjoy the evening. Look for me at the conclusion of the event and I shall take you back to the wharf."

Nelson touched the man on the shoulder with a pat, slipping a handful of coins into the man's open hand. "And thank you again," he said with a smile.

Their escort stepped back to the carriage as his hand weighed the coins. He climbed back aboard and called to his horses to pull away.

The group showed their invitations to the front guardsmen.

"Ah, our distinguished guests. It is an honor." The man extended his hand in welcoming.

They exchanged handshakes, and after a brief conversation of politics and current events, Nelson led his men into the courtyard.

As he moved forward, Ben noticed two figures walking toward the open doors where the reception was to be held: one was a man clad in the distinguishable colors of the Royal Army, the other, his escort, in an elegant dress. The gown's train puffed out on either side, trimmed in silver and blue. For a moment his eyes strained to catch a glimpse of her face, but then he lost sight of her gorgeous blonde hair through the rush of other guests.

✖✖✖

As Nelson and his officers entered through the arched doorway, a pair of event workers hailed the group for their seating arrangements.

"Your name, kind sir?" said a friendly-faced old man.

"Arthur F. Nelson," the captain said, "And my three officers." He recited their names.

The man behind the small table looked at a chart and black placards with names written in golden lettering. His old eyes peered through the bifocals that hung loosely on his nose. "Ah, yes. Absolutely wonderful! Our honored guests! It is with great pleasure that I make your acquaintance."

The four men smiled and nodded.

"Well, here you are now," he said, reaching for the card. "You will find your seats in Section Fourteen," now pointing to the diagram.

Nelson eyed the man's bony fingers. "So, the king's table faces the guests?"

"Yes, you'd be on the king's right-hand side, the first table inward from him. There are fourteen sections total, four guests to a table, numbered clockwise."

"Ah, thank you," he nodded at the two Englishmen. "And what of our covers?"

The friendly man smiled. "You can leave your hats with my partner." He motioned his hand to the man beside him. "We'll hold them for you until the light show outside is about to begin."

"Until then, my friend," Nelson replied.

✺✺✺

They maneuvered through the corridors of the building, passing through halls laden with items collected during the reign of the king's grandfather, George II, as well as of the many that had ruled before him. There were paintings, rugs, framed memorabilia; it seemed as if they were witnessing Britain's long and celebrated history unfold with each footstep. One last doorway separated them from the large room housing the reception.

A man stood at the entrance to the grand room, greeting the visitors. As Ben entered, he stared around, bewildered at the scene that surrounded him. Of the fourteen sections, about half were already occupied by distinguished noblemen, officers, officials, and their female companions.

As the clock showed quarter to seven, several more groups of people arrived, filtering in through the entrance toward their assigned seats. No one talked as all eyes were on the large clock that hung above the grand fireplace, at the rear of the king's empty table. Now, all sixty-four guests were seated as the clock struck seven; all waiting anxiously for the king and the royal family to emerge from doorways located on either side of the fireplace.

A man emerged from a shadow, walking in front of the king's table, directly at the center of all the guests. "Good evening. My name is Edmond Don Lorenzo, and I would like to proudly announce the arrival of the royal family. It is with great honor, in which we dine tonight together. If you would all stand …" he trailed off as he maneuvered through the gap in the tables nearest Nelson, cutting the corner, and coming to stand before the fireplace.

Inside the fireplace, a pile of stacked wood sat atop a metal grate. Beneath the grate sat gears and pulleys, arranged in a specially requested, custom design. With a pull on a lever located at the foot of the fireplace, hidden behind a beautifully carved marble statue of Venus, gears would shift, turning a series of pulleys that slowly tipped a bucket of water. Beneath this bucket sat a large cube. The spots where the water dropped sizzled into a mist that slowly filled the surrounding area.

Simultaneously, an upper tier of gears turned, sending a circular disc of rigid flint to strike against a steel file. The sparks set blaze to the dry kindling located throughout the wooden pile. The flame quickly caught and began to spread deep into the wood itself.

✖✖✖

The audience began clapping at the spectacle, still anxious to view the arrival of the Royal Family. Ben peered at the clock once again, noticing that only a single movement of the minute hand had passed since his last observation.

"This is so exciting!" said the wife of a colonel sitting a table away.

The husband nodded with anticipation. All eyes were on the growing fire and the thick smoke that rose vertically into the chimney.

✖✖✖

As the water soaked the cube, the chemical reaction began its process and white smog began to rise, billowing upward through the grate. The blades were angled inward into the room, sending the thick foggy blanket toward the audience. The blanket of smoke thickened as the seconds wore on, displaying a dazzling effect to those witnessing the event. To the common eye, this billowing smoke looked to be caused by the spreading fire.

Several shrieks volleyed between tables; there were a few who thought the blaze would spread ever further. Un-oiled hinges squeaked loudly as the doors opened. Figures slowly emerged, walking through the blanket toward their table, which was engulfed by the thick fog.

Distinct sounds were heard over the crackle of the fire and the gasps of the audience. The sounds of chairs being pulled back and the weight of bodies sitting on the wooden carved chairs sliced through the smog. These sounds teased the spectators' senses. After five minutes, the thick fog slowly receded back toward the fire, as another series of gears opened to vent the area.

A series of gasps were heard as the scene unfolded before the sixty-four guests. Each member of the royal family lay face-first atop the table, dead.

Don Lorenzo lay sprawled out by the fireplace, as if he had tripped over his own feet in an attempt to flee the havoc caused by the fire. As the guests closest to the Royal table began to push away from their chairs to rush to their king's side, a loud sigh echoed through the large room, as one by one, each family member came to their senses.

Don Lorenzo stood up and cupped his hands around his mouth. "And without further ado, I give you King George William Frederick the Third and his wife, Lady Charlotte of Mecklenburg-Strelitz!" the man stated with a cheer.

The audience roared with laughter at the prank, for most held the mindset that the entire royal family had died before their very eyes! Among the family members who joined the king were Lady Amelia Sophia Eleanor, Sir William Augustus, Lady Mary, Lady Caroline Matilda, and several cousins; including fifteen-year-old Lady Louisa Ann, who stood off to the side. The latter stood tall and proper, displaying a brilliant smile for all to see. She knew all eyes were either on her cousin King George III, or herself. She was beautiful in every sense of the word and unmarried, having hundreds of offers to marry into the royal bloodlines. Her red dress was elegant, but simply made. It wasn't too flashy, but at the same time, she captured the attention of all of those in attendance.

The tapping sound of spoons on glass brought the audience from their loud clapping to silence.

"Thank you all for attending. It is with great pleasure that I find myself dining with so many wonderful people. If my distinguished guests would stand and be recognized for their bravery." He paused, allowing Captain Arthur F. Nelson and his officers to stand. King George III introduced the uniformed men to all. "At the conclusion of tonight's celebration, I shall present you with gifts for your heroic duties to King and Country."

A loud cheer filled the grand halls. "To King and Country!"

The noise subsided as Don Lorenzo stood before the crowd. "The first course of the evening will consist of a plate of roasted turkey and geese, basted with butter and dredged with flour. Also on the menu will be carps in corbullion. To complement these will be fricassee of turnips, white soup, oyster sauce, and a salad with a gentle yet smooth dressing. At the conclusion of the first course, I shall again inform you of the dining options. But to continue, once the third, and final course, is cleared, we shall then proceed to the ballroom floor for some dance. After listening to the music of George Frederick Handel, there will be a light show in the courtyard through which you traveled earlier."

The king then sat down, followed by his family, and finally by all of the guests. A line of servants as far as the eye could see, came out one by one from a doorway that linked the kitchen and the ceremony room. They were dressed in common serving attire. Within only five minutes, each table was covered with a bounty of fresh food and drinks.

All eyes were on King George III, awaiting his signal to commence eating. He spread a large silk fabric over his thigh and into his lap, preparing for the meal. The others followed his actions, and once their ruler began eating, the sounds of forks and knives scraping against the plates interrupted the silence between chewing and small talk amongst the tables.

✖✖✖

Ben looked up from the dishes that covered the table in front of him. He licked his lips and began eating.

Through a mouthful of food he managed to speak. "Captain, did you try the fish yet?" He turned his head to his left, glancing past the other two officers.

Nelson focused his gaze on his youngest officer. "No, not yet, but the roasted turkey is most outstanding. How is it?"

Ben finished chewing before speaking. "Out of this world."

"I concur," Nate Brodkin added.

"The soup is a bit salty, but other than that it's great."

The group continued to comment on each course between mouthfuls of the delicacies. After several minutes, most of the guests began looking around at the interior of the State Ballroom. A series of stained glass windows lined the upper portion of the room, letting in the last rays of daylight. Above the guests' heads were three columns of golden chandeliers with their candles flickering brightly.

Ben's gaze traced the curves of the candelabras that were spaced along the very outermost edges of the room. His eyes were focused on the red walls, unable to determine the material that seemed to create a wavy illusion. A huge carpet spread across the entire dining area. Noticing the different patterns and stories that had been sewn into the ornate carpet, he smiled.

A familiar face popped into his mind, and he began imagining Leah, with her blonde locks of hair, in the empty bowl that sat atop his empty plate. He then stared out across the gap, directly at table one. The four guests of that table ate silently, with content and delighted expressions. His view moved from section to section, taking in the vast array of colored dresses, suits, and uniforms. The first three sections contained just couples in their later years of life, dressed elegantly and gracefully, politely conversing to pass the time.

The first man of the fourth section wore the colors of the Royal Army, and bore a somewhat aged face. Ben guessed him to be in his early thirties. The man's red hair stood out like no other he had ever seen before. The fire-like locks were greased back into a tight ponytail. Ben felt the hairs on his neck rise at the man's sight, but not out of disgust. Though good-looking in features, the man gave off a rather unpleasant aura that Ben could sense from across the dining arrangement.

Next to the uniformed man, his young wife stared silently into her plate. From where Ben sat, there were several decorative candlesticks that obscured a full view of her face. He studied her smooth skin and how the flickering flame brightened her luster, adding to what he could see of her beauty.

Ben blocked out all other targets in the crowded hall; his sole focus was now on Leah. She leaned forward, reaching for a drinking glass with an open hand. Emerging into his view was the gold medallion that hung around her neck. He remembered the gift he had given her on his departure from Grand Bahama many months ago. A smile formed on his face as he realized he had not been completely erased from her memory.

His hand moved to the collar of his uniform, feeling for Leah's gift. He pulled out the locket from against his chest and held it in his open hand, staring at the small painting inside.

Ben's attention was drawn to Don Lorenzo as he stood to address the guests. "The next course consists of ragout of celery with wine, fricandos of veal, and vegetable pie."

The line of servers then tended to each table, removing all the plates, utensils, and glasses. Minutes later, the servers reentered with the second course and new dishware. Using white gloves to carry the hot trays to each table, the food was distributed to each set of four guests.

✖✖✖

Time passed quickly and an air of happiness spread through the grand hall. It was time for dessert; the distinguished guests each digging into the bowls of freshly picked fruit, nuts, and plates of rout drop cake.

Leah glanced around from table to table, curious as to the differences in how each guest dressed and how they carried themselves. She presumed that the average guest in attendance was between thirty and forty years of age, and there were several older couples. These elder men had been in the councils and in Parliament longer than some of the younger guests had been alive.

She remembered her husband had mentioned the names of the honored guests. As each face changed differed table-to-table, she noticed one younger gentleman with attractive features focused solely on a gold locket. She studied Ben. His hair was longer and his face clean-shaven, but other than that, he seemed quite similar to that young man she had once known in what now seemed to be another life.

Ben ran a hand through his hair, letting several strands fall over his brow. As he replaced the locket back beneath his shirt, he felt a pair of eyes on him. Trying to locate the origin, he sensed her warm smile radiate toward him from across the room.

❉❉❉

Musicians tended to their instruments, tuning strings or playing short tunes, as the king invited the guests toward the dance floor. A conductor raised his hands high in the air, preparing to start the music.

"Ladies and gentlemen, may I present to you the London Baroque Orchestra."

With a wave of his hand, the man behind a grand piano began a series of slow and repetitive octaves as he moved his hands from left to right. His foot touched the pedals at the end of every measure, setting the pace for the introduction of the song.

Violins and other stringed instruments came in shortly thereafter. The guests moved to the dance floor for a waltz. Nelson and his three officers moved to the side, where the king stood with a content smile as his guests listened intently the music of Handel.

"Are you enjoying yourselves this evening, gentlemen?" the king asked.

Nelson gripped the man's hand firmly, shaking it as he looked into the eyes of his sovereign. "Yes, I think I can speak for everyone; the food was outstanding and the drinks were quite refreshing."

"My staff and servants were chosen as the best from around the world and this musical assemblage is delightful as well," the king replied.

"Yes, I agree. They are quite delightful," Nelson said. "If it pleases you, may I introduce my officers?"

The king smiled. "It would be an honor to meet such outstanding protectors of the Crown." He shifted his gaze to the man closest to Captain Nelson. "You are?"

The first officer bowed his head. "Charles Marconi, at your service."

"Nate Brodkin, serving as second officer."

Ben beamed a large and friendly smile; he was shaking hands with a man he had learned about in European Studies, but now here he was, living the history rather than reading about it. "And I am Benjamin Manry, sir."

King George III looked at the young man before him, studying his strong features. The officer before him was just a lad. Ben was a teen in the middle of that difficult transition between boy and man, on a quest to find himself and his very purpose in the world. "May I ask your age?"

"Yes, sir. I turn eighteen on the Fourth of July."

With a shocked look on his face the king paused to comprehend. "And you've made third officer already?"

"Yes, sir."

"How long have you been working under Nelson?"

"Sir, it's been almost six months since I joined his ship near Grand Bahama, with my brother and best friend." He decided to omit a majority of the truth behind the statement.

"You must tell me of these adventures, I've only heard them through the press, and you know what they say about that. I'd prefer a firsthand account anyways."

❌❌❌

The music continued as pairs gracefully moved across the dance floor. King George III motioned to his young cousin, Louisa Ann, with a wave of his hand. She came to his side quickly, with a wide smile.

"Your majesty, the banquet is extravagant so far! Are you enjoying yourself, my dear cousin?"

"Yes, of course I am. I throw the most exquisite parties." He winked with humor. "I noticed you standing aside. Would you care to dance?"

"Of course." She beamed a smile.

Their hands extended as the two began the waltz, dancing to the melodies of the orchestra. They moved across the ballroom floor, observing those around them. "Louisa Ann, may I ask you something?"

"Certainly, my king."

"What do you think of the young lad over there." He eyed the corner where the four uniform clad officers stood. "Would you like me to introduce Ben to you?"

She smiled. Her eyes practically devoured Ben from head to toe.

"Yes!" She paused taking in the view. "I would like that very much. You are too good to me, dear cousin."

The king laughed. "Nonsense, I would do anything for you, and you know that. How is the search going? I know you are still looking for a suitable husband."

"Well, I suppose I am still looking. But we shall see." Her eyes were glued to Ben across the ballroom.

✷✷✷

Through the couples crowding the dance floor, Leah saw Ben enter the rectangular area. For mere seconds at a time, she managed to spy Ben and his dancing partner across the ballroom floor. Captain Highmore noticed her wandering eyes.

"Darling, is everything okay?"

She shook her head. "Yes, yes of course."

"Good," he replied as they continued their waltz.

Ben appeared once again, this time in clear view, but his face was turned sideways, as if he were searching for something as well.

✷✷✷

"Dear cousin, this is Benjamin Manry, acting as third officer under Captain Arthur F. Nelson." King George III finished the introductions.

"Pleased to meet you, Lady Louisa Ann," Ben said with a smile.

He studied her mass of flowing dark hair, then his gaze shifted to her curved lips. Though her eyes were soft lavender, she held Ben with a piercing gaze that took the strength out of his legs. He felt weakened by her presence. Her stature reflected how well she presented herself; her confidence was as high as the clouds.

"The honor is all mine," she said as she held her dress to curtsey. Her gaze continued pressing Ben for something further.

He was unsure of how to progress, but felt compelled to say something.

"Would you like to dance?" Ben asked shyly.

"I would be a fool to refuse such an offer." Her cheeks filled with a rosy color.

They waited for the next cycle to begin. Seconds later, Ben's outstretched hands found Louisa Ann's and maneuvered to the center of the floor. The couple joined the remainder of the guests. Looking over his partner's shoulder, he saw Captain Nelson engaged in conversation with the king, as Charles Marconi and Nate Brodkin stood a few feet off to the side.

His gaze moved to the young lass who stood before him. Her blush subsided as she slowly became accustomed to him. Her gentle lavender eyes gave off a desirable aura that could only make Ben smile.

✖✖✖

The song came to an end, causing the hall of guests to still for the break. They talked quietly for a minute before the conductor began the next piece. The man waved his wand quickly, as cellists and violinists seemed in competition as to who could play faster. Then pace slowed considerably after the first ten seconds, with the introduction of a steady rhythm from the man at the grand piano.

Ben glanced around for a few moments, looking for the one his heart longed for, but to no avail. Instead, he looked down at Louisa Ann's wide smile and felt guilty.

He stared into Louisa Ann's eyes, hoping that the focus would put aside thoughts of Leah. "Are you having a good time?"

"Yes, I am. You dance marvelously." She teased.

"Really?"

She giggled. "Yes."

They continued dancing until the song ended. There was a short delay as the conductor readied the musicians for the last song of the evening.

When the music resumed, the dancers continued moving elegantly across the dance floor. Once the tune ended, King George III stood beside the conductor. All eyes moved toward their country's leader.

"I hope you've all enjoyed the orchestra. If you would all please return to your seats now, I would like to commence the award ceremony," the king announced to the joyful crowd.

✖✖✖

All eyes were on King George III and the four men who stood before the audience. The king cleared his throat and then raised a glass of wine to his lips. He took a long swig and then swallowed.

"Ah, the lovely taste of a fine wine!" he called out for all to hear. His audience laughed. "I now introduce Captain Arthur F. Nelson, master of the HMS *Defence!*"

The king waited for the round of applause to fade away and then spoke yet again. "Arthur, it is a pleasure as always." His loud voice boomed for all to hear. "Wear this award for your dutiful services to King and Country."

The crowd cheered in response. "To King and Country!"

Ben watched as his mentor moved forward to stand before King George III. The two shook hands and then Nelson allowed the king to slide a hand under the lapel to pin on the award above many other merits the captain had obtained over years of dedicated service. The audience applauded once Nelson's stood at attention before King George III.

"And now, Charles Marconi, serving as first officer under Captain Nelson, and in command of the beautiful HMS *Courtesy*."

Charles shook hands with Nelson and then the king. He snapped to attention and then allowed the king to pin on the award. As before, the audience clapped and he stood beside Nelson and King George III.

"And now for the second officer, Nate Brodkin," the king called out as Nate moved forward, leaving Ben alone at Table Fourteen.

The king repeated the procedure with Nelson's second officer and then there was a pause in the ceremony.

"And last, but certainly not least, is our young Benjamin Manry, serving as third officer under Captain Nelson," the king called out.

It seemed as if all eyes were glued to the youngest officer of the lot.

Ben walked to where the king stood and smiled. He snapped to attention and shook hands with the four men. As the pin was being fixed to his uniform, he stood tall and proud, puffing out his chest boldly.

"This concludes our pinning ceremony. Let us now formally meet, and proceed to the courtyard. You will be provided with masks for the masquerade event outside."

✖✖✖

*L*eah sat uncomfortably beside her husband. She had been waiting anxiously to get a chance to talk to Ben alone, but it seemed as if that would never happen. The king raised a glass in salute and then took a long draught of the wine. She watched as one by one, Nelson and his officers came up for the award ceremony. Time slowed as

Ben made his way to stand beside the king and his fellow shipmates. She beamed a large smile at seeing the love of her life stand tall and proud, eagerly awaiting the award that King George III was about to pin to his chest.

✖✖✖✖

Louisa Ann sat amongst her family. She had felt several stares on her throughout the night from several older and unmarried gentlemen, particularly while dancing. She had countless offers of marriage, but she did not wish to marry for money or for land. She was young; she wanted what any girl her age wanted … love, or at least a similar version to it. As Benjamin Manry stood before her cousin, she felt a sudden sense of warmth spread throughout her, starting in her heart and radiating throughout her body.

✖✖✖✖

The guests organized themselves by section, individually greeting the royal family in line. Nelson and his three officers began their series of handshakes and friendly smiles.

"My king." Nelson nodded. "I have yet to see Prime Minister George Grenville in attendance."

"We shall speak of business at the conclusion of the evening," the king said quickly to keep the exchange at a minimum.

Nelson nodded, "Yes, your majesty."

Ben beamed a hearty smile as he shook the king's hand again and then continued down the line greeting the hosts. When Louisa Ann bowed her head in curtsey, a smile came to her face as Ben presented himself.

"Why, hello Mr. Manry, I was not expecting to see you again."

Ben smiled. "And how are you, my lady?"

His words had a powerful effect, causing her to blush a deep red.

Nelson nudged him forward and continued toward the remaining members of the royal family. Since they were the last section to be met, the other sixty guests were already situated along the side-wall.

For the next several minutes, guests introduced themselves by their names, ranks, professions, and anything else that they felt should be shared. All ears were open as governors told of their mansions and estates, as lawyers spoke of how they handled their most famous cases, and as authors spoke of their latest writings.

✖✖✖

"Robert? Robert Clive!" Charles Marconi broke from the group, moving forward to greet a man he hadn't seen in several years. "And Margaret! It is so great to see you!"

Ben studied the man who stood before him, noticing the bifocals that hung loosely around the man's neck. With a closer inspection, Ben noticed the numerous medals and ribbons that decorated the man's Royal Army uniform. A sash crossed from his left shoulder to his right hip, leading to a sheathed sword. Ben's eyes then moved to the man's wife. She was wearing a pearl-colored dress, and displayed a bright and friendly smile

"I was excited to hear your name announced earlier, my friend." Robert smiled. "It's been quite a while Charles, I've not seen you since March of 1760!"

Marconi nodded and replied with a laugh. "Aye, it has been a while!"

Robert let out a hearty laugh. "Aye, that it has. We've some things to discuss! How have you been since last we spoke?"

"Well, much has happened. I was assigned to Captain Arthur F. Nelson." He paused and turned his head to make sure that his boss was ready to be introduced. "Here he is."

Nelson extended a hand to the man. "It is a pleasure to meet you."

Charles continued. "Arthur, this is my friend Robert Clive, First Baron of Plassey, and his wife Margaret." He paused. "Robert, Margaret, this is Arthur F. Nelson."

Robert smiled, shaking the man's hand. "It is a pleasure to meet you! If you're a friend of Charles, you're a friend of mine!"

"Pleased to make your acquaintance." Nelson placed a friendly hand on Robert's shoulder. "Let me introduce you to my other officers." Nelson motioned for Ben and Nate to step forward. "This is my second officer, Nate Brodkin, and my third officer, Benjamin Manry."

"Gentlemen, I am pleased to meet you both. It is a great honor," Robert paused and then looked at Ben. "You are young! How old are you?"

"Seventeen, sir," Ben smiled proudly, aware of his accomplishments at such a young age.

"That's exciting! You've many years ahead of you." He paused, preparing to change the subject. "You may not be familiar with what I've done, but my admirers know me as the Conquerer of India. I was in charge of the East India Company and we fought in the Battle of Plassey. I've decided to stay in England for the time being as a statesman, currently in search of reform for the East India Company."

Ben took the lead, speaking on behalf of his fellow officers. "Delighted to meet you. You may have heard of our last mission, of battling the famous pirates *El Perro Loco*, Blood Spot, and his cousin Captain Blood Bones."

"Oh, yes! That most certainly rings a bell. Have you met Captain Richard Highmore yet? He's a good friend of mine. He was also stationed in Bombay, India during our struggles with Holland, Spain, and France in the Seven Years' War. He's got some grand stories about our invasions there. I'm sure you will become acquainted with him soon!"

Ben extended his hand. "Again, it was a pleasure."

Captain Nelson shook Robert's hand and led the way to the next group, headed by a large landowner in York, as well as a member of High Council. The eight members chatted for a while, as the women stood back to let the men conduct their exchanges.

✖✖✖

*A*gain, the groups rotated, meeting new people, sharing stories, and shaking hands in greeting.

"Good evening, I am Captain Richard Highmore." The man offered a firm handshake to Nelson. "May I present my wife, Mrs. Leah Highmore."

"Nice to meet you. I am Captain Arthur F. Nelson," These are my officers: Charles Marconi, Nate Brodkin, and Benjamin Manry, respectively."

"Ah, gentlemen," Highmore said, bowing his head. His red hair was slicked back into a neat ponytail. He extended a hand to each of them in turn.

Leah stood motionless. Her eyes met Ben's, and their gazes were glued to each other.

"Hello, Ben," she mouthed the words, but barely anything came out.

A twinkle in his eye gave way the joy that radiated inside his chest.

"How are you?" Leah's words finally formed, though the process seemed to take forever.

"Good, I'm … really good. I'm first officer aboard the HMS *Courtesy*." The news of his recent success seemed of little importance in relation to the fact that he was finally standing in front of her again. He paused to collect himself. "I thought I'd never see you again! I even went to your estate after we finished our last mission, but you had already left for England. Your mother said I'd just missed you," Ben said, prodding for any sign of emotion, or a glimmer of hope.

Their voices were hushed, barely loud enough for the other men and women around to hear. The two captains moved to the side to chat, as Marconi and Brodkin stood with their hands on their lower back, their stances impressing a nearby formidable banker and his young wife.

She frowned, clearly upset at hearing of their near miss. "I thought your mission would have only taken a month or two. What happened? I was hoping to see you again before I went off on my own little adventure." She craned her head to look at her husband.

He relayed the story of all the mishaps that had occurred.

A look of suspicion settled on her face. "Are you telling lies? Or are you just telling me a story of a dream, perhaps?"

He let out a laugh. "No, it's all true, every word of it! I would never lie to you. You know that. Tell me what is going on with you."

"I know, but that story is hard to believe!" She smiled; content to be in the comforting presence of Ben again. "Well, after you left, I went to the cave and beach nearly every day, hoping you'd come back soon." She closed her eyes as she began reliving the memories. "I then began the countdown to my eighteenth birthday and my inevitable marriage. He's a gentleman and a good enough man, but I had no choice in the matter."

Ben looked over Leah's shoulder, witnessing the grin on her husband's face as he continued to check on their conversation. "Don't look back, but your husband keeps eyeing us."

"Let me tell you, I am quite used to it. If I talk to anyone for longer than a few minutes here and there, I feel like I am always being watched, whether it's by him or that eerie feeling you have when something is out of the ordinary. I just wish I could get away from it someday and be alone."

"I might be in town for a few more days before the next mission starts, maybe we could meet up?" He paused for a moment, and then teased, "Or, you could sneak out, and we can run away together!"

She shrugged. "Well, I do not know if that's such a good idea, but we shall see," she said with a growing smile.

✖·✖·✖

The guests filed out through the halls, retrieving their jackets and hats from where they'd left them earlier that evening. Once the items were restored to each individual, a handled black mask, inlaid with gems, was given to each guest. A sole white feather atop the mask distinguished a male owner, while two green feathers meant a female. A long line of guests walked down a marble staircase, emerging before the grand fountain surrounded by a series of candles and lanterns. The line split in two, dividing around either side of the octagonal fountain, filling in the courtyard space.

A team of specialists fiddled with fuses, readying the rockets and fireworks for the light show. King George III walked to where the men stood. "Are we ready?"

A man nodded. "On your call, your majesty."

"Good. When I finish my speech, you may begin." The king moved toward the fountain, with his sentries motioning to the guests to clear a path. He climbed atop the outer edge of the fountain, stood tall and called out. "After a splendid evening of music and delicacies, prepare for the next event of the masquerade. Please, don the masks provided and enjoy the light show!"

As he stepped down to the ground, the first series of fireworks were sent skyward. The explosion above the guests sent colors of blue, orange, and red in fizzled streams outward. The crowd began to cheer as the sounds of violins echoed across the courtyard. Eyes looked up toward the roof. The entire orchestra had began yet another song.

Behind their masks, guests moved around the fountain to the tunes and the series of explosions and flashes of lights, dancing without a care in the world.

✹✹✹✹

Louisa Ann stood beside her cousin as he signaled his men to commence the light show. She craned her head around, looking at the rooftops and at the orchestra above. She smiled, enjoying the night as another song began. She thought Ben had passed in front of her so she moved from the king's side in pursuit. She took a detoured route by moving around the fountain rather than following in his wake. She walked without delay down the marble steps and began her quest, eager to dance yet again with the young man who seemed to be perfect for her. As Louisa Ann continued around the fountain, Ben nearly knocked her over in his own pursuit of someone else.

❌❌❌

*B*en caught sight of the silver embroidered dress and tracked Leah, maneuvering through the crowd of people. As he approached, she had her back to the fountain, and her fair skin caught the moonlight, radiating an ethereal glow.

"And what are you doing?" Leah asked with a playful smile.

They noticed how each other's bodies moved to the music; the graceful progression of tunes and notes echoing through the courtyard causing their limbs to stir in turn.

"I was just thinking of asking you a certain question of large proportions and of great importance," Ben responded with a smirk that nearly spread ear to ear.

"Oh, really? And what would this grand question be?" Leah countered.

"Simply put, may I have this dance?"

The mask hid her large smile. "Um, I suppose I would allow that."

They touched hands and danced to the lively music, spinning in circles and then swapping partners with those closest. After several partner-swaps, they found themselves enjoying each other's company yet again.

❌❌❌

*L*ouisa Ann watched as Ben locked fingers with the young blonde introduced to her earlier as Leah, the wife of the successful Captain Richard Highmore. Her gaze split the crowd and solely focused on the couple dancing in their own little world. They were lovers; she could tell by the way their eyes were locked upon each other. Louisa Ann felt a pain sear through her heart as she looked on from a distance.

✖·✖·✖

*A*s the last of the fireworks fell earthward, the music stopped. Another grand speech followed and the king thanked all those in attendance for the being part of the celebrated occasion. Lines formed as the king bade each group farewell. Captain Nelson and his officers stood off to the side, letting the remaining guests flow past, just as the king had instructed them to do earlier. Once all had left the courtyard, King George III waved the four men over to his side. As a group they proceeded to his private quarters for their meeting.

✖·✖·✖

*W*alking arm in arm, Richard Highmore escorted Leah to the awaiting carriage. He noticed her glimpsing one last time into the courtyard. He opened the carriage door and allowed Leah to enter. As he stepped in, he craned his head, looking back at the faces of Benjamin Manry and his fellow officers.

"So did you have a pleasant time, Leah?"

She nodded. "Yes, it was all exquisite. Did you enjoy yourself?"

"At times. That lad, what's his name?" He paused, building up the tension. "Um … Benjamin Manry; he seems like a swell lad."

She nearly fell for the trap, but carefully held her tongue. "Yes, that he does."

"Have you ever seen him before?"

Not knowing how to respond, she simply replied. "Yes, he's … an old friend."

The darkness inside the horse buggy shadowed her smile at the mention of his name, but also masked her fear, knowing that her husband had brought up the topic for reasons she could only guess.

9

June 21, 1763
King's Quarters
Buckingham Palace, London

The group of five stood inside the warm, cozy quarters. It had been a lovely evening with all in attendance complimenting the affair. Ben stood beside Nelson and his fellow officers, aware and eager for what the king had to say. A fireplace crackled in the background, adding to the tension that filled the air. All were thinking of the next mission, and what it would bring to the officers and their men.

"Gentlemen, sit down and relax. Did you all enjoy your evening?" King George III asked with outstretched and inviting arms.

"Yes." Nelson signaled his officers to be seated. "We found it to be a most pleasant experience. Thank you as always." Nelson bowed slightly and then sat in the remaining chair.

"Of course. How could I let such an assortment of heroes go unnoticed?"

The comment brought a smile to the men's faces.

"Before I dismiss you for the evening, there is important business to discuss concerning the next mission and what it requires of you." His eyes stared at each individual officer. "You've been told little so far due to the extreme importance of the task, but I shall now describe to you the details of what I desire."

They moved to the edge of their seats, eagerly anticipating their next set of orders.

"As you know, the prime minister and I have differing views, on, well nearly every issue. The snob even refused to attend tonight's event because he had other less important obligations. He is ignorant in everything he does! Ever since he took office he has done nothing to benefit us. His heavy taxation in the Colonies caused an uproar that I alone have to deal with. I've asked him to step down from his position countless times, but to no avail. No matter what I do, or can do, it is quite nearly impossible for him to be removed in the traditional sense of the term …" he trailed off. "This is where you four come in."

He began describing what he wished to happen, first as an outline, and then in more detail as he poured several more rounds of wine through the night. At the conclusion of the third bottle split between the five, King George III stood up lazily.

"So, what is your answer?"

"My king, with due respect, may I have a word with my officers before we continue?"

The king blinked, stunned at the hesitance in Arthur's response. "Yes, yes of course."

"Thank you. Should we leave the room?"

"No, I have to use the washroom. I shall return in a moment. Hopefully you have an answer upon my return."

King George III stood, and quickly exited the room. Once they heard the door close, the officers turned in their seats to face each other. Charles Marconi was the first to speak.

"I don't like this, not at all." Marconi shook his head.

Nate Brodkin nodded in agreement. "Sir, do you realize what the king requests?"

"Of course I do, Nate, Charles." He only mentioned their names because Ben remained silent, staring into the knuckles of his interlocked hands. Nelson eyed Ben for a moment, prodding into the recesses of his newest officer's mind.

"Captain, this would be considered treason," Ben said without moving his eyes from his lap.

He looked at his youngest officer. "Yes, it could be thought of as such, but it fulfills the wishes of our king, and our sole duty as privateers is to see that his very wishes are fulfilled."

"Even if it means *taking* Grenville *out of office?*" Ben countered, emphasizing the importance in the meaning of the phrase.

A slight wrinkle at the corner of his mouth showed hesitation and doubt. "We must do this." Nelson glanced at his first officer before continuing. "If we succeed, we have accomplished all of our assigned missions. Gentlemen, consider this our last mission together. We can then retire to our homes, see our families, and enjoy the lives that we are destined to live."

✖✖✖

The officers stood upon the king's reentrance into the room.

"Have you come to a conclusion then?" King George III asked as he motioned for the men to take their seats once more.

"Yes, we shall take on this mission with the utmost haste. I will write you of the plans to come, and then once again," Nelson paused, looking for the right phrase, "on the outcome," he finished. Though a confident and extremely capable leader, Nelson struggled knowing there were several factors outside of his control.

✖✖✖

Louisa Ann stared deeply into the mirror. She had just taken a hot bath and was now brushing her hair. A large bath sheet was wrapped tightly around her chest and covered her well past her knees. Beads of water dribbled down her hand as she moved the brush through her thick, tangled black hair. Thoughts from earlier in the day came at her in a rush. Three faces seemed to appear comingled: the face of her cousin, King George III, that of her newfound love, Benjamin, and lastly, that of his lover, Leah.

"Ben will be mine, somehow or some way. My cousin will help me, whether he is aware of my intentions or not. From this moment on, Leah will no longer play a role in his life." She promised herself in the flickering candlelight. Her eyes transformed from luscious lavender to an unnatural red, consumed by a hatred that let a crooked smile fill her beautiful and innocent face.

✖.✖.✖

Nelson rubbed out the crust that had formed around his eyes as he usually did on late nights such as this. He could not sleep; thoughts of the next mission filled his mind. He weighed each possibility for planning and execution, but was still stuck. Every new idea seemed to have some loophole.

"What if we fail? We are already well known from our previous endeavors; therefore we are connected to the king as his right-hand men. That wouldn't be overlooked in Parliament; people would notice. This must be well thought out, well-planned and well-executed."

Nelson continued, listing possibilities in his head until he couldn't count all of their angles and aspects. He heard the ship's bell ring out the time; another four hours had passed on this sleepless night. Pacing gingerly around his quarters, he opened the exterior doors that led to the balcony on the stern of the vessel. It was here where he'd often look clear his mind. After a therapeutic session of breathing in the fresh air, he found himself back in his quarters, staring yet again at the journal entries of Captain Blood Bones.

August 14, 1751

> *It has been nearly a week since I last scratched the quill to the parchment inside this crimson journal. Much has occurred since I joined up with Carlos Torres del Salvado, the man I met in the tavern. I was quite surprised to learn that my cousin, Álvaro, was also a member aboard La Monzòn. On the third day, departing from the port of San Juan, we engaged a Spanish flute, lightly*

guarded by a sloop. All available hands lay along the bul-
warks with our knives and swords at the ready.

With all the hatred I had for the greedy Father Sala-
dino, as well as the backstabbing Captain Bernardo Ber-
mudez, I waited, anticipating the glory in which I would
soon find myself. We had two things in our favor; a small
complement on deck visible to our prey, and a barrel fire
with a large quantity of whale oil, rubber, and pieces of
tarred cloth. The fire released a vast amount of a blackish-
hued smoke that rose with the light breeze.

The two vessels came close, probably to investigate
what had happened. When we lured their ships in, we
shot several volleys of chain, felling a number of their
sails and tackles. Within minutes, our helmsman came to,
cutting directly between the two Spanish ships.

Our men rose together as one, and those of us on the
portside raided the merchantman, and those on the star-
board wrecked havoc upon the unlucky little sloop. They
surrendered within half an hour, sustaining numerous
losses while we only lost several brave souls.

I smiled with our victory, carefully balancing sor-
row and contentment. I knew what I was doing had no
impact on Father Saladino and Captain Bernardo Ber-
mudez, but for now, it was just a temporary rung on a
ladder that I was destined to climb.

Nelson set the journal down in his lap, thinking of the late hour
and how time had seemed to slip by while he continued to further
his knowledge about the man he had just recently captured and seen
put to the gallows. Tomorrow would be demanding: a day full of
planning, talking to the right people, and consulting with his officers. But the stories of Blood Bones, or rather, the transformation
of Hernando Audaz into the fearless pirate now heralded as the infamous Captain Blood Bones, was something he simply could not
pass up. Nelson smiled at the brilliance of the deceptive plan he had

just read about and then dove yet again into the alluring world that had been painted in beautiful detail.

September 3, 1751

Several weeks have passed and several ships have been taken in the name of the black flag that we fly from our mast. I often think of the life that I'd be living if I had never walked into my commanding officer's quarters early, witnessing the event that had taken place on that night, a night that seems so long ago. I would have probably been promoted several times by now.

But that is all in the past, and now I must concentrate on two things: the present, and the future.

I met an interesting fellow, a man of sorcery, and not those tricks of hand or light that I have seen commonly displayed in the streets of Madrid or Barcelona, but rather of the magic of mages and witchcraft. I felt that I had been introduced to Merlin himself. His name is Sesostris and we all called him the Egyptian. I can only fathom that was where he was from.

The man was in his mid to early fifties, though I could only presume so on my first glance. The wrinkles on his face carried scars that led to many stories, stories that he told me during our meals together. He was the cook, and soon became my mentor in our after hours. He took my cousin and me under his arm as we raided and plundered the seas for all that they were worth, and if I were to tell the glorious truth, the seas were bountiful, for I soon found my purse laden with gold.

I knew my family would look down on the lifestyle that I had chosen to live, my father a viceroy, and my mother a wealthy noblewoman, but ever since I had escaped from the dungeons of El Morro, I had not once thought about returning to the rich and lavish life that I once knew. I found my new path of life … exhilarating.

Nelson's eyes were tired and heavy. In mid-sentence, his forehead touched his outstretched forearm and he fell into a deep sleep. Not once throughout the remainder of the night did he stir. He dreamed of Blood Bones and George Grenville, and the outlandish request that King George III had made.

10

June 22, 1763
London, England

The sun rose, sending beams of brilliant light that filtered in through the open porthole into Ben's quarters. While the room went from dark to light within half an hour, he awoke slowly. He remained there beneath a blanket, recounting all the dreams that he'd had throughout the night, trying to make sense of some of what had seemed unusual. One dream seemed to stick out above all others as he stared at the overhead.

He was being chased down a corridor that emitted no light. This eerie darkness hid the barren walls that he ran through. There was some mysterious force that was breathing on the back of his neck. When he turned his head to see if the pursuer had gained, it was too late.

The "thing" had closed the distance and then reached out, and their two bodies united as it clung to his back and began sinking its long, sharp fangs into the soft flesh of his neck. It was hard to describe, but the one thing he recounted in detail was the color of the monster's fur. It was fiery red. Ben shivered.

Ben remained motionless, unmoving as the visions flashed before his eyes once again, trying to analyze what had just occurred in his dream.

Stretching, he sat up and then placed his feet lightly onto the wooden planks. Taking in several deep and trancelike breaths, he was ready to start a new day. He pulled on fresh socks and breeches and walked toward a water basin that he had filled the night before. Dipping his hands in, he washed his face and then dried off with a washcloth. He reached into his sea bag of washed clothes, placing an undershirt over his head and then continuing to don the rest of his uniform. He smiled; remembering the night he had shared with someone new, as well as with someone from what seemed a former life.

✖·✖·✖

Louisa Ann looked across the table to her cousin, the most powerful man in England. After chewing a mouthful of eggs and swallowing the first course of breakfast, she beamed a large smile. "My king, last night was grand; the food, the music, and the company. I could not have asked for a better time."

He nodded, recounting the many conversations and comments he had received at the event's conclusion. Then his thoughts wandered to those of Arthur F. Nelson and his officers, men who had bravely served him in prior years. He prayed that they were ready for what soon lingered ahead.

"Yes." He paused, noticing Louisa Ann in a trance. "It was a rather remarkable turnout. As always, our entrance was memorable." He looked around the table at his family. "Do you wish to say something more, Louisa?"

Her mouth was forming words, but she was inaudible to the family members that filled the room. "Well. It's just that over these past months I have been introduced to so many men; men from well-known families, men from rich and noble families, men from both England and abroad, but none have met my fancy. None simply have found a place in my heart." Her words sank in, and all waited anxiously for what was to follow. She bit her lower lip, excited by the deliberate phrase that would soon escape her mouth. "That is, until I met Benjamin Manry, the young lad you introduced me to and that I danced with."

Obviously Ben was a man beyond his years, seventeen and acting as third officer under the respectable and unfailing Arthur F. Nelson. The king nodded. "I did see tremendous potential with him. He is younger than all of your suitors, much younger and handsome, very kind and warm-hearted. He is a man who has accomplished much in such a short matter of time. He seems that he has great things lined up in his future."

"Yes." She smiled and forced a blush to turn her cheeks crimson. "That is why I am telling you all this now. I wish to see him again," she batted her long eyelashes, winning the crowd over as easily as a skilled puppeteer masters his strings.

"If that is what you wish! Oh, you will, Louisa Ann, but in due time. I've some business to tend to and for that simple reason he will be leaving soon."

Her face dropped. The king noticed this, and then smiled. "All right, I suppose we can invite him tomorrow for brunch and to spend the day at the estate." Looking around the table at his fellow siblings, wife, and other relatives, he continued. "Does anyone object to Louisa Ann meeting with a potential husband on the morrow, a man whom I trust and respect dearly?"

❈❈❈

The officers met in Nelson's quarters aboard the HMS *Defence*. Breakfast was brought out in silver serving dishes, platters used for important occasions such as this. Without procrastinating, Nelson cleared his throat.

"Gentlemen, you all know why you're here."

His three most favored subordinates nodded. He continued.

"We have to assassinate Prime Minister George Grenville. We have to do it secretly and soon. This puts us under escalating pressure, for we need to think of an detailed plan, and then analyze the risks associated, and finally, execute it."

His men nodded once more. All remained silent as they watched Nelson pause strategically to build the suspense in the air.

✖✖✖

*H*ours had passed as they dissected options, weighing risks and advantages to each.

"Men, we will meet again tonight for a late dinner. My brain cannot fathom any more planning. Take the rest of today for your individual pleasure. Enjoy London and all that is in it. Ben, I know you had mentioned that you need a supply of ink. Charles, I know you wish to return home, being that it is only a day's ride away, but we must take care of business first. Lastly, Nate, go enjoy a performance at the theater, for I know how much you like that," he said with a joking wink.

The men erupted with laughter.

"And my dear captain, what of you?" Nate asked in the midst of returning the joke. "I'm sure there'd be an available seat next to me in the theater. From what the ladies say, you most certainly enjoy theater, and after that, we can go take a stroll along the mighty Thames and, if the evening warrants, skip pebbles."

Nelson stared at him with a grin.

"Oh, that sounds exquisite! And tea time afterward?"

"Ah," said Nate with a growing smile. "I wish to enter a tavern and not leave it for the majority of the day."

Nelson shook his head. "Nate, Nate, Nate, what are we to do with you?" A smile grew on his face. "So be it!" He then looked at Ben. "Is this your first time in London?"

Ben had been quiet for the majority of the morning, only answering questions directed at him. "Yes, captain."

"Ah, I see. And what are your plans for the day?"

Ben thought for a moment, letting his brain sift through the ideas that were entering his head.

"I'd like to see the Tower of London, the bridge, and definitely spend a relaxing afternoon along the Thames." He looked into the plate for a few moments, and the yolk of an over-easy egg transformed into the familiar golden curls of Leah, and he smiled at the thought of having seen her the day before. Before continuing, he shook the thoughts out of his head. "And what about you, sir?"

"Most likely running some errands around town, we have to refit the ships again with fresh water and other stores. You know how things can go; you can never be too sure."

Charles nodded. "Yes, you're right."

Ben and Nate chipped in with an "Aye".

They finished talking, then placed all the silverware on the top plate after stacking the four dishes. "Ben, can you do me a favor and bring this back to the scullery?"

"Of course. Is there anything else you need?"

The captain glanced toward his youngest officer. "Let me think. Yes, come back to my quarters once you finish; I have something else for you."

"I'll be back shortly, sir."

❌❌❌

Ben peeked into the open doorway, eager to hear the request from Captain Nelson. Perhaps it was one of those quests he'd always dreamt of doing — something far fetched, like traveling to some far away place, fighting a dragon, rescuing a princess, or something along the classic lines of adventure.

Nelson looked up and waved him in. "Yes, take a seat."

He paced forward, standing tall, with chest out, representing a proud example of a uniformed man.

"What is it you need, sir?"

"Well, two things. First off, if you need any reading material, I found several volumes of journals during our recent expeditions. Blood Bones was quite the character. I've read through about a half-dozen entries. I'll let you read them once I'm finished. I also need you to deliver a note to a personal friend."

Ben smiled. "That sounds great, sir. Of course, just tell me where to go."

"The man's name is Peter Bailey. He lives in a house opposite Kensington Palace and Gardens. It will be a red shingled, three-story home, with a marble patio. The house number is 214. Keep the Thames on your left side, going westward. Follow the river along the embankment, past the Square, the center of London, and go up a side street called Ingrid Hill. I believe that's the shortest way. Follow this road for quite some time. The moment you think you've gone too far on it, just keep going a bit further. You'll see the Palace and Gardens on your right hand side. Peter's house will be on your left."

Ben nodded throughout the directions, visualizing roads he'd never traveled, paths he'd never trekked. And in the end, an adventure awaited, even if there were no dragons, princesses, or far-off places.

"So, Benjamin. Do you think you can handle it?"

His visions changed from scenes of castles and princesses to the sharp features of a clean-shaven, serious-faced Arthur F. Nelson.

"Yes, of course. Is there anything else you need?" he said with a serious face.

Nelson let out a hearty laugh. "Ah, Ben, I knew fate had intervened when that storm brought you, Sal, and Harris our way. Yes, I am certain stars have crossed for some unknown reason. I couldn't have asked for a better lot of men."

Though only words, Ben could grasp his sincerity by the man's expression.

"Thanks captain, that means a lot."

And with that, Ben was dismissed. He left the captain's quarters, feeling as important as he ever had. He seemed to hover, walking inches over the ground.

❉❉❉

"So, what do you guys want to do?" Harris asked, looking at each member in the group.

"I could definitely go for some good food," Sal chimed in, nodding at Jacob.

"Yeah, you could always go for some good food," Ben said with a smile. "It has never stopped you before."

"Funny, I notice how no one laughed at your joke."

On cue, the three friends laughed, pointing and smiling at Sal. Jacob heartily slapped his thigh.

"Oh, well aren't you the jokester," Sal replied.

The laughter faded away as they stood together slowly, moving away from the bollards that lined the pier, and began their second day of adventure in London.

"Where to?" Harris asked.

Ben hesitated before answering, interrupting Sal's plea for food. "Nelson asked me to deliver a personal note to a friend of his. So before we go off and explore, I should take care of that first."

"Oh."

"Yeah." He looked at his brother. "I don't know if you guys want to come with, or if you just want to meet up later." He paused for a moment and then looked at Sal. "Sorry to ruin your food parade."

Sal nudged him with a friendly elbow. "Eh, I think I'll live a few hours without something in my stomach."

They followed a series of piers and docks that led out from the dockyards, like a group of soldiers ready to conquer the world. Spirits were high as they began exploring the nooks and crannies of London, England.

The views that Ben now took in were different from those of the scenes that flashed before his eyes the night before in the horse-drawn carriage. With the help of the sun that trickled through the clouds above, and the casual pace at which they meandered along the Thames, they walked besides brick houses scattered along the river banks, towers that pierced the sky, and countless people going about their normal business on the warm day.

"Wow, London is nice!" Ben called out to no one in particular.

Harris looked at his younger brother. "Yeah, I couldn't agree more. It's kind of neat to get to see something we've only learned about in class. If only that cursed treasure had brought us to ancient Egypt or some place cool like that."

"Why Egypt?" Sal chimed in.

"The pyramids, the Sphinx; why not?"

Ben smiled. "I think Harris is right for once," he said. "It would be pretty neat, but we still don't really know how the curse works yet. I mean we are stuck here in eighteenth-century England, at least for the time being."

"Thanks for the update there; I could have sworn we'd just fought off a wooly mammoth with spears, fighting next to half-naked cavemen." Sal smiled.

"Sal, although that would be pretty damn awesome, no. No, no, no! Seriously, what did you do in a previous life to deserve such a bad sense of humor?" Harris replied with a huge grin.

Jacob, the quiet one of the group, broke out into laughter as the elder Manry commented last. All eyes turned to him.

"About time you opened your mouth," Harris said. "For a moment I thought we had left you on the pier."

"I'm sorry, I'm just taking everything in," Jacob replied. "It's quite different from Grand Bahama. I haven't really traveled much."

"Don't worry, man," Ben said, slapping Jacob's shoulder. "This is new to us too."

✹✹✹

Ben noticed that the buildings began to get closer together; back yards were also someone else's front yards, and likewise business stoops were shared. The friends stopped in the center of the city, pausing as they moved toward a series of marble benches.

"Let's take a seat for a bit. I'd like a chance to sit and just look around," Ben said.

The group nodded in agreement.

"Yeah, that sounds relaxing. It's surely a nice day out," Jacob said. "So, after this letter delivery, what do you all want to do?"

"Well, I think if we had made a right out of the shipyard, instead of the left we made, we could approach the London Bridge and a few other neat sites." Ben paused. "When I was talking to Captain Nelson it didn't seem like everything was that far away."

"Oh, all right." Jacob smiled. "That sounds great."

They sat there on the white and gray marble bench for ten minutes, absorbing the culture and the living history that continued to pass by them. London accents carried on the slight breeze, as they listened in on several conversations of those who passed nearest.

"Blimey! Did you hear what she said about him?" A lady dressed in a stitched garment of rags said to a friend.

"Indeed, what nerve did she have? Let me tell you, if she'd ever say something like that to me …"

Her friend responded with a laugh that made Ben quiver.

"Oh yes, would you and Chester like to come this evening for tea?" The lady asked her friend.

Ben nudged his friends. "Let's get out of here before we hear any more soap operas unravel. One thing I definitely don't miss from back home is afternoon cable TV dramas."

The group let out a hearty chuckle as they continued down the street, soon finding the path that Captain Nelson had described in the briefing. Ahead, they saw groups of people wandering through the streets, with their bodies angled as if they were all gazing at something.

"Wait, I think the Kensington Palace and Gardens should be coming up soon," Ben informed the other members of the expedition party.

"What's that?" Jacob asked.

"Not a clue," Sal replied.

Before realizing it, Ben began reciting random facts and trivia, "William III bought the original land, I think in the late 1680s or sometime around then. He liked the location so much that he had someone design what is now Kensington Palace. After that, Queen

Anna or Anne, I think that's her name, well, she enlarged the gardens. Four decades later the wife of King George II, Queen Caroline added the Serpentine and Long Water."

Harris looked dumbfounded at his brother's recitation. "How the hell did you know all this random trivia?"

"Ha! It's ironic, but I was watching some show a few days before our little *adventure* began. It was all about London and its surrounding sights."

"Oh yeah, I remember you watching that."

"So, anyway," Ben paused, then looked toward the left. "Yeah, it should be over there coming up."

They walked for another five minutes as the gardens on their right began to blossom into full effect. A kaleidoscope of color filled the courtyards: dark reds and light oranges, intense blues and gentle violets, and landscape greens and bright yellows. Grand statues and majestic fountains lined the areas surrounding these beautifully decorated and well-kept gardens.

"Wow," they said in unison.

Then the palace came into view from where it had been hidden behind a mask of dense foliage, miles and miles of hedge mazes. Ben eyed the iron and gold gates surrounding the huge building. Through the gaps in the gate's bars, he could make out several fountains lining the walkway to the beautifully adorned main entrance.

"Come on guys, let's deliver this letter," he paused, staring at the palace. "I want to get this job done so we can just walk around and explore," Ben said.

"Yeah, yeah, yeah!" Harris smiled at his brother. "You know how I am with sightseeing."

Jacob and Sal listened intently as the two brothers were about to begin yet another friendly argument.

"Harris, you only go sightseeing if you see girls, and this time, you're seeing English girls."

His cheeks flushed a reddish hue. "And your point?"

Sal chuckled. "Guys, guys, we get cursed through the perils of time to 1763, and nothing changes?"

"Apparently not." Ben altered his steps, heading toward the other end of the street.

They continued walking in silence, counting off the paces in their heads. By now, they had come perpendicular to the front gate of Kensington Palace. The sun had reached its apex in the sky, marking local apparent noon.

They stood before a well-kept wooden fence that surrounded Peter's property. The lawn and hedges had been trimmed recently, and a wonderful rose garden lined the stone walkway that led to the marble patio. On the outside, Peter Bailey's home seemed small in comparison to the grand display of wealth on the opposite side of the street.

11

June 22, 1763
London, England

After a series of knocks, Ben thought he had heard a shuffling sound behind the oak door before him. In his peripheral vision he noticed a shadow shift the lavender colored drapes in the house's front window. A nose and a pair of eyes under heavy bifocals peered out, investigating the guests at his doorstep.

A moment later the door creaked open and the man's full figure emerged into view. Though it was only a few minutes past noon, he was dressed in a casual robe, light blue in color that was wrapped around his upper body, secured with a bowtie. Nearly hidden was a pair of beige trousers. His feet found comfort inside a pair of light brown moccasins.

He studied the four young men who stood before him. "Good afternoon lads."

Ben smiled in return. "Good afternoon, sir. You must be Mr. Peter Bailey?"

"Yes."

He reached into his pocket, and pulled out the wax-sealed letter. Ben then handed it over to the man who stood relaxing against the front door.

"Sir, here you go."

Peter eyed the unique seal, knowing who had penned the note.

"Come in, come in!" he said, waving the group inside his warm home. "And how is dear Arthur?" he said with a growing smile. It had been a long while since he had seen his friend, the master of the HMS *Defence*.

The man turned on a heel, leading his four guests through the spacious entryway that passed by a large staircase. Once inside, a warm wall of air hit Ben in the face. He could smell the fireplace in the sitting room toward where they were walking.

"May I interest you in any refreshments?" he asked his guests. "Please, take a seat and get comfortable."

Jacob was the only one to reply. "A cup of tea, perhaps?"

"Yes, yes of course. And for the rest of you?"

"We'll have the same, please." Grateful for his host's generosity, Ben looked to the others, indicating for them to sit.

The man walked over to the small wooden stove, opened the door and stared into the embers. "Ah, let me just place another log on."

Silence prevailed as he made his way toward a stacked pile of wood that rested inside a large copper trunk. His hand touched the topmost log, gripping it just underneath a large knot. He then placed it atop the burning flames, waiting for it to catch. Unsatisfied with the position, his hands found the handgrip of a poker. Sticking the pointed end in, he adjusted the logs until he saw the new wood begin to smoke.

"Ah, about time," he muttered, but loud enough for those around to hear.

"Is there anything we can help you with?" Ben asked, sensing a slight frustration in the man's last statement.

He hesitated for a moment, as if going through a mental checklist. "Yes, my servant has been sick the last few days so I gave him off so he could rest. It's nice not having to be waited on day and night. But I suppose if I'm making five cups of tea, we should fill the pot a little more."

"All right, sir."

Ben moved to the man's side and grabbled the teapot.

"The kitchen." Peter pointed to another doorway in the room. "Is just over there. You've got to pump about ten or so times to build up the pressure. It will flow as if there was a river running right through the pipes."

✖✖✖

*W*hile the remaining figures sat, Peter slipped a finger under the wax seal and began reading the note from his friend:

> *Peter,*
>
> > *It has been quite some time since I have had the pleasure of enjoying your company. I wish to speak with you as soon as time permits. It is grave and important. My latest mission can only be described as nearly impossible. There are so many factors I must to consider, but I know that between you and I, we can conceive a plan and complete the mission in the allotted time.*
> >
> > *I cannot go into the details now, for if this letter were to somehow be discovered, it could mean a death sentence for all those involved. If you can return to the dockyards for an evening on my ship, the HMS Defence, either in company with my third officer Benjamin Manry, or by yourself, I would enjoy the visit.*
>
> > *For King and Country,*
> > *Captain Arthur F. Nelson*

✖✖✖

*L*eah lay beside her husband at the very edge of the bed. She looked around the room as her eyes adjusted to the light that slipped through a break in the curtains. She got up and moved to the window, careful to not awaken her fiery-haired husband. Placing her hands on the sill, she peered out through the glass at the surrounding London landscapes.

Instead of traveling back to their estate in Brighton the morning after the banquet and masquerade, Richard had decided to take lodging at an inn along the River Thames. He had told Leah that they would be staying there for several days as a getaway, but even in the brief amount of time they'd been married, she knew that it meant other things. He would be gone for a majority of the day meeting with friends and diplomats. This meant one thing for her: she could roam London like she'd always dreamt of doing, to explore the historical city firsthand instead of hearing stories from her parents and family friends.

After a quick breakfast of fruits and buttered toast, she sat on a sofa beside her husband as he began to pull his leather shoes onto his feet.

"I'll be gone for most of the day," he said, not looking at the beauty that sat beside him.

"Oh, all right," she said, pretending to be disappointed.

"Yes, business as usual. What do you have planned for today?"

She hid a smile. "Eve and I talked about going for a long walk along the Thames and then stopping at a small café for lunch."

He concentrated on tying the laces before he responded. "Oh, that sounds lovely."

With that, he stood, stretching his back before he turned to face her. She stood to meet him, and he took her hand, kissing her hand like he always did. The two had yet to discuss children or even acted upon it. Their marriage had so far been in name only and their relationship restricted to polite gestures.

Normally her face would redden, but today, there was only one thought that cycled through her head, and that was of Ben.

She wanted to see him. She had to, because if she didn't soon, she knew that their paths might never cross again.

❧❧❧

Captain Nelson scanned his quarters for sloppiness, readying for Peter's arrival. He had sent out the invitation in a letter delivered by his young third officer. In the hour that had passed since he'd granted the crew liberty, he had cleaned off his chart table, organized the many bookshelves and cabinets, and even swept the lovely decorative rug that sat comfortably in the middle of the room.

Bored, he paced to his desk, sitting down with a sigh of contentment at having been productive. He grabbed the familiar crimson leather binding, spreading the pages open to where he had last left off. His eyes skimmed through the previously read words, then skipped a page until he found the next entry.

October 5, 1751

We've taken five merchant ships this past month, without counting their half a dozen escorts. I have talked to the mage named Sesostris. I have read through several personal volumes that he has let me borrow, and between the two of us, we've spent many hours after the sun has met the horizon in the ship's study talking late into the night. He has taught me many languages, which he tells me broadens my worth.

I also have taken the time to approach the captain and learn all I can. He has shared some of his techniques with me over the last few days. It seems that every discussion tells of a tactic that he has used over the years; for example, entering a harbor under a neutral flag and snooping around, seeing what ships are worth attacking. We have deployed this tactic several times and it always works.

I looked at the chart's noon fix, and it seems like we are island hopping on our way for Jamaica, the capital of piracy. From what I've heard in the holds, it seems like certain adventure looms ahead.

I'm currently sitting in the crow's nest, viewing a patch of dark clouds that encompass the ship. It looks like rain will soon come, so I must head below to the comfort of my hammock.

Nelson reread the journal entry. A somewhat unexpected feeling came over him. He found himself obsessed with the life and travels of Blood Bones. This ritualistic action of opening the crimson journal and then diving in headfirst, being completely overtaken by the stories, seemed to have become as natural for him as breathing. He placed the book in his lap, letting the journal close. Nelson reflected for a moment, absorbing the pirate's words and seeing if any could be helpful for the upcoming mission.

There was a knock on his cabin's door.

"Yes, yes. Come in."

A sailor's face popped in. "Sir, I'm just letting you know that the starboard side gun ports are freshly painted and look good, but we decided to not start on the after doghouse. It just started to rain. I don't know if you've looked outside lately, but the sky has changed for the worst. The clouds are getting thick and much darker."

"Let me have a look," Nelson said as he put down the cursed journal and followed the young seaman out of his quarters.

✖✖✖

"Michael, follow Leah from a distance," Captain Richard Highmore commanded. "She will venture off and explore the city with Eve as she told me, that I do believe. But I do not know if she secretly plans to meet up with a young man named Benjamin Manry. He is an officer under Captain Arthur F. Nelson. I have heard of their past meetings on the island of Grand Bahama before we entered wedlock, but I sensed something between them at the masquerade, and I shall soon end whatever it is they have. She is my wife now, and regardless of whether anything had happened prior to our courtship, I can only think of what is now and of the future," he paused, letting his speech carry to his man's ears. "And in this future, Ben does not exist. Mark my words," he let out a booming laugh. "I will end Benjamin if it is the last thing I do!"

His fiery hair parted as he ran a hand through it, creating the illusion of a dazzling display of fireworks atop his head.

"Yes, Captain Highmore. I shall keep a close eye on her, and follow in the shadows. Do you want me to do anything about this Benjamin you speak of?"

He shook his head, his fiery locks dancing. He no longer had his hair tied back in a tight ponytail, but rather had let nature take its course. "No. It is not the time for that. I wish to learn what he is about and break him from the inside. I fancy getting inside his thoughts and ruining him, taking everything that he has and destroying all that he holds dear, even if it means hurting my precious Leah."

"Understood sir, I shall leave at once."

✹✹✹✹

*B*en pumped ten times and then waited. Soon water began to flow through the pipes and into the sink's drain. Quickly he angled the teapot under the flowing water, filling it to the top. He soon joined Peter and his friends in the sitting room.

"Here, take a seat," Peter said, looking Ben in the eyes. His warm and friendly smile shone brightly as his hands reached out to the teapot. The young visitor handed the kettle over.

"Thanks for everything, sir," Ben said once he was sitting comfortably beside Jacob on a two-seat sofa.

His eyes took in the beautiful adornments of the sitting room; carvings, statues, and paintings seemed to cover every square inch of the walls, books littered the shelves, and Oriental rugs and the skins of rare animals lined the floors. Beside the sofa was a wooden end table made of cherry with a large scrimshaw ship in its center. On the table sat a pile, neatly stacked, of saucers and cups with near-matching designs. Beside the pile, several spoons were laid out on napkins.

"You're quite welcome. You may all call me Peter, though, there is no need for any formality," he replied with a smile. After a slight pause, he continued. "Benjamin Manry, please introduce me to your acquaintances."

He thought it odd that the man already knew his name, but being a friend of Captain Nelson, he wasn't surprised with how much he knew. "Peter, this is my brother Harris Manry, and our friends Sal Draben and Jacob Hughson."

"Much obliged," Peter answered. "Please tell me about Arthur. How is he faring as of late?"

Each filled in a portion of their story. Peter's jaw dropped as the tale spiraled together in detail.

"Amazing, s-simply amazing." His English accent stuttered for a moment on the words. "And when'd you get in?" He already knew the answer, but he noticed how much his guests loved to tell their stories from their own differing points of view.

"Just yesterday, on the summer solstice. We were the distinguished guests at the king's banquet and masquerade," Ben exclaimed enthusiastically.

"That's magnificent! Would you care for another cup of tea?" he asked as he noticed a circle of the tea remnants under the stirring spoon in his own cup.

Ben looked at the grandfather clock that stood tall and proud between a drawing desk and a globe of the world, mounted atop what seemed to be a pyramid of carved ivory. His eyes took note of many circles of ink around the globe.

Peter noticed Ben's transfixed gaze. "Ahem." He cleared his throat to get the lad's attention. He smiled. "You're probably about to ask if I had spilled a vial of ink on that globe over there?"

Ben answered with a nod.

"Well, I'll tell you what. I will put on another kettle of tea, bring out some fresh pound cake that I purchased yesterday, and then I shall tell you all a grand story."

Several moments passed before Peter had rejoined his guests. "So, where was I?" He strategically paused; building the suspense for the story that would follow. "This is a tale of the building camaraderie between Arthur F. Nelson, and the very own Peter Stanton Bailey, myself if you wish." He paused yet again, smiling as the four listeners inched forward in their seats.

"We met in 1759. We left Bristol sailing towards Guadeloupe. Commodore Moore was in charge of our mission and along with Arthur and a good friend named Victor Smith, we led a bombing of Basse-Terre, Guadeloupe on January 23, 1759 ..." Several of the man's words went over Ben's head as a similar story came to his mind.

"Where have I heard that name before?" Ben thought.

"... After a successful bombing, Major General Peregrine Hopson led an invasion of the city. The men fought with indescribable courage. After spending several months on the island, a tropical disease spread through our camp. General Hopson fell ill and died, on February 23, 1759. During the three-month long campaign, we captured city after city. The first of May was the turning point, where the French surrendered Guadeloupe. The three of us were then assigned to the French island of Marie Galante. Maybe later I'll show you all some weapons that I captured from an officer when the island fell on May 26 ..."

Ben drifted off again and recalled the conversation he'd had with the captain about the battles he had fought prior to their previous mission.

"... So after Marie Galante, Arthur and I were shipped to Montreal, while Victor stayed in the Caribbean. Arthur and I saw limited action in the Colonies, but he was then shipped back to the Caribbean." Peter scratched his head for a moment. "That was in the first few weeks of 1762. I stayed in the Colonies, undertaking various missions between governors. After a few months of service, they granted me leave and I decided to move back to merry ole England. I found this lovely lot, built myself a home and now call it my own, using funds that I had earned over the years. I then learned of Admiral George Rodney and Arthur's success in conquering Martinique in the months leading up to that summer. News had been sent back, just several days after Rodney and the captain had laid siege to Havana. Victor stayed in Havana, where I believe he still remains, and Arthur — well you know what he has accomplished."

They nodded. "Yes, I think Captain Nelson met up with him when we were there," Ben replied.

"I haven't seen either one since we all went separate ways. I'm looking forward to coming to the ship tonight for dinner. I've got some business to tend this afternoon, but I will be seeing you later on this evening."

"That sounds great."

"Yes, yes of course, but I'm not kicking you all out of my house just yet, unless you have other things to tend to. I don't get visitors that often, so I'd love to continue the conversation."

"Well, we were just going to walk around London for a few hours and then head back to the ship," Ben answered, knowing he would be doing the man a favor. "We can keep you company for a while."

He smiled. "That would be great."

Peter stood to his full height, stretching after being seated for a length of time. Though not old in age, his body had endured countless tolls during his service to the Crown. "If you'd like a tour of the house, I can certainly entertain you with some of my collections …" he trailed off as he began walking forward with a slight limp in his right knee.

He made his way towards the kitchen, but stopped a few feet short. Placing a hand on the right-hand side of the walkway, he felt for a small lever. Gripping the end piece of a railing, he gave it a slight tug. There was a clicking sound as gears turned inside the well. With his left hand he pushed in a side panel.

Before entering, he craned his head back. "I'll show you the exciting things first." A smile formed on his face as he spoke the phrase, hiding something from the others.

Once the man entered through the gap in the panel, Ben paused for a moment, letting the distance increase, just out of his whisper's reach.

"Guys, where do you think he's going?"

"Who knows and who cares!" Sal looked at Ben, keeping his excited pitch as low as possible. "Maybe some hidden room or some top-secret British governmental facility."

"Yeah, he's right," Harris said. He shot a quick glance towards Sal as if to shut him up. "It doesn't really matter."

"All right, I am glad that is settled then, let's keep going!"

Ben increased his pace, closing the distance with Peter. To act as if he had been there the whole time he cleared his throat. "So where are we heading?"

"Just wait and see," Peter said with an air of mystery.

Through the outstanding architecture, light was able to enter the corridor from above, almost as if a sunroof had been constructed for that sole purpose. Pacing several more feet, Peter came to another stop. Unlike the other areas of the house that they had been to so far, this corridor was bare of ornaments, with the exception of wooden panels that were layered with dust.

"It's just in here," Peter continued.

Ben angled his head around the opening. The paths were only shoulder-wide, barely enough for one-way traffic. They then came to an opening. Above their heads were ninety-degree angled boards that led upward.

The space above their heads began to dwindle, causing them to duck underneath the overhead boards. Pausing beside yet another wall, the man's hand reached for groove in the panels. Gripping a circular inlaid gear that stuck out of the wall just a few millimeters, he pressed it in and then turned clockwise. Another panel swung open and he stepped through. The trip had taken at least five minutes as they had zigzagged underneath the main floor through dark corridors that were barely lit.

"And here we are!" He opened his arms widely, pointing back to the entranceway of his home.

The group of five stood before the doorway as if reliving their earlier greeting.

"Why did we just go in a circle?" Ben mumbled the question in puzzlement.

A smile formed on Peter's face. "Just thought I'd build the suspense for what's to come." He laughed at the conclusion of the statement.

With that, he turned on a heel and began his trek up the wooden staircase. After reaching the landing between the first and second floor, Peter paused. Once all stood beside him, he cleared his throat. "Are you all ready?"

He continued before anyone answered, climbing the staircase to the second floor. Without stopping, they soon found themselves at the third floor of Peter's home. In the main hallway of the third floor, they passed by several paintings of battlefields and clipper ships. At the end of the hallway, there was a sole circular window, bare of any curtains. The mid-afternoon sun filtered in, warming the floorboards beneath their feet.

"Ah, what a beautiful day," Peter said as his hand felt for the doorknob to the room beside the window.

"Yes, it is," Harris said quickly, eagerly awaiting what was inside the room.

Peter sensed the edge in the young man's voice. Delaying yet again, he stopped the door's swing, only revealing a minuscule view of the room's interior.

Ben saw the smile on Peter's face grow larger. "At least he's getting a good kick out of this," he thought.

"Finally, here we are," Peter said with a gentle and prolonged bow.

He at last pushed open the door, exposing the room's contents to their eager eyes.

They proceeded to a grand table that took up the majority of the room. Ben's gaze was solely focused on the tabletop's contents:

mounds of dirt and patches of grass, trees and bushes, and small painted soldiers. From the doorway the distance and angle disguised the tedious work that had been put into each and every detail. Upon closer inspection, Ben noticed two different colored uniforms on the soldiers that stood on the battlefield.

"What battle does this depict?" he asked, looking for a name-plate as he thought aloud.

"This, my friend, is what I saw at Marie Galante. This is my version of what happened. After our victory I had a long discussion with one of my comrades and he suggested that I pick this up as a hobby. It sounded like a grand idea so I decided to try it. I then began sketches in the days that followed the battle so I would remember each minute detail."

He pointed to each area of the dirt and grass battlefield, tracing circles and arcs around contingents of men.

"This was my company. We held down this area for several hours in a standstill. Finally, after we saw an opening, or rather a weakness in the enemy's foothold on this hill, we struck with a devastating blow," he paused, knocking down several enemy model cannons and troops with a sweep of his hand. "We took the hill and then flew the flag of Britain, giving our fellow troops hope of the soon-to-come victory."

The guests smiled and nodded, knowing he had put so much time and effort in reconstructing the battle.

"I spend too much of my time in here as it is, there's no point in wasting your time as well."

Ben shrugged it off. "It's all right, it's a neat hobby. I used to build models, when I was," he paused, not wanting to offend his host, "back home. I haven't been able to continue doing it since I joined up with Nelson."

"I'd love for you all to stay and chat with me more, but I sense your friends are a little jumpy." His eyes moved from Ben, studying the anxious young men who were eager to start exploring the cityscape of London.

"Well, see you, then?"

"Aye. Tell Arthur I'll be coming for dinner if you see him. It was a privilege to have met you all." He bowed his head, escorting them out of his house.

12

June 22, 1763
London, England

Uniting flesh and stone, Leah's hand softly touched the wall that ran throughout London's entirety. Built by the Romans around the port town of Londinium, she could feel its history enter through her fingertips, flow through her veins, and enter her brain. The result was a radiant smile. She slowed her gait as her eyes took in the scenery; meanwhile Eve kept a few paces distant. Leah spotted an arch in front of her as a horse-drawn carriage emerged from one of the medieval gates. Long ago the wrought iron bars had protected the roadways leading to the old countryside, but these were later removed to allow ease of transit for the populace.

Leah paused for a moment, allowing Eve to catch up. Thoughts of possibly meeting up with Ben raced through her mind as she explored the city. As much as she loved Eve's company, she longed for only one person's presence.

"Eve, if you don't mind, I would like to go off and wander alone for a little while," Leah said with a genuine smile.

Eve nodded and then curtseyed. "My pleasure, madam. If I know you like I think I know you, I believe you wish to come across a certain someone." She teased.

Leah retorted with a chuckle. "Nonsense, if it happens it happens, but until then I shall see you when I return back at our lodging."

Eve waved goodbye as Leah turned around, navigating westward through small side streets along the northern bank of the River Thames, her feet adjusting to the slight upward slope in the terrain. Emerging into view were the four turrets of the White Tower. From far above, she could hear the cawing of ravens as they circled one of the turrets, evidence of a recent public display of gruesome death in the protected courtyard. The turrets soared at ninety feet high.

Leah stood unmoving for a few minutes, taking in the sight before she continued walking. She kept the Thames on her left-hand side for an hour, stopping periodically to sit and look at the mother geese that had their flocks in tow. It was a beautiful day, warm and sunny. She exhaled with excitement at the feeling of this newfound freedom she felt, able to explore something new without her overprotective husband Richard around.

✹✹✹

*B*en took the lead, his friends falling in line behind his quick and excited pace.

"All right, if we backtrack for a few minutes, I think we'll be able to find everything we talked about earlier. Let's get some food, I'm a little hungry," Ben announced as they walked down the street.

"I could go for some food!" Sal smiled.

"Yeah? You can always go for food, my non-fat friend. On the way back to the ship though, I'd like to check out a general store. I'm out of ink, and I'll probably need some other things."

"Yeah, me too," the others chimed in.

From behind, they heard the clopping of horse hooves against cobblestone. Ben looked over his shoulder, watching as a team of carriages rushed by. The sounds of men and women talking as children played filled the bustling streets. They continued their hurried pace, anxious to view new sights. The adventurers easily lost track of time as their gazes wandered randomly through the streets with no particular destination in mind. Red-bricked stores clogged the thoroughfare, marking the beginnings of the business sector.

"Wow, London is really nice," Sal said.

A group of young women passed by, their umbrellas warding off the sun's rays.

"And the ladies are beautiful, and bountiful!"

Ben smiled. He knew his brother; nothing changed even while lost to the perils of time.

"Wow, if I wasn't dressed in this naval uniform, I would've thought we were still in St. Augustine, walking down Main Street, after watching a movie …" Ben trailed off.

Sal smiled, awaiting the next line or even a possible retaliation from Harris.

"… Chasing down women like the beast of a man you are!" Ben called out.

"Oh, brother. How you slay me!" Harris replied with the hint of a smile on his face.

"I guess we should get you a girlfriend." Sal laughed.

"Ha! Look who's talking, Mister-I'm-Afraid-To-Talk-To-Molly Wiggins." Harris returned the tease.

"She's in love with my dancing ability! We boogied down hardcore at the Freshman Halloween Dance. We made a good combo: Princess Leah and a Blood-Sucking Vampire."

Ben shook his head. "Dude, do you realize those two don't go together at all? Star Wars meets Count Dracula?"

Harris let out a laugh of victory.

"What I meant is that we looked good together. I wish I could've just asked her out."

All of a sudden the prospect of never returning home dawned on them all. Their moods quickly soured.

Jacob had been waiting to say something throughout the discussion. Sensing an opening, he jumped at the opportunity. "Well, just wait two hundred years. Then ask her to be yours!"

Three pairs of eyes stared at Jacob, who was known for his silence.

"Wow, I thought I heard someone say something. Perhaps it was the wind?"

Ben looked at his brother. "Or, maybe the sound of another passing carriage?"

Sal laughed. "No, I really think Jacob spoke. Aw, baby's first words! But, I'll admit, that was pretty damn good!"

Jacob smiled. The four continued walking, laughing at life's follies as they explored the nooks and crannies of the network of entangled streets. From a distance, Ben noticed blond curls rustling in the wind. He immediately became unaware his friends had made a left into a tavern. He continued forward, his gaze glued to the person walking his way.

"Hey, come on!" His brother's voice snapped him back from his daydream.

Ben looked over his shoulder. "Yeah, hold on. I thought I saw Leah."

"Oh, she's here?" Harris called through the doorway. "I thought she was down in Brighton with her other lover."

"Shut up dude, that's not funny! No, I saw her at the masquerade and I met her husband. I really don't like him."

"Of course not; he stole your girl!"

"Harris, geez. No, he just gives off an evil vibe. I got a bad feeling about him, but that's beside the point."

"Well, was it her?"

He returned his gaze to where he had last seen the golden locks. His eyes strained; separating families, stragglers, and marching soldiers. Through a sea of faces he looked, but to no avail.

❦❦❦

Nelson and the ordinary seamen stared off into the calm waters of the harbor. The sky seemed to clear the moment he got on deck; thick, dark clouds thinned to a near white as the sun shone through, warming his face.

"Honest sir, I swear it was raining the moment I went to tell you."

"It's all right, lad. I appreciate the information; we can never be too sure, even when in port. Weather can change just as quickly as our own fates do. I will be having company tonight, so please tell your relief that Mr. Peter Bailey will be joining me in my quarters for dinner. Have the cook bring down a fancy meal for us, with plenty of wine to quench our everlasting thirst."

"Yes, sir." He smiled at Captain Nelson's requests.

✖✖✖✖

As Leah came to an intersection, a large storefront window appeared before her. She could see her body clearly in the reflection, along with the reflections of many other people that were in the streets. From the corner of her eye, she caught a glimpse of a figure in a dark robe. She looked over her shoulder. The shadow was nowhere to be seen.

She picked up her pace as she began to feel uncomfortable. She felt the presence of her follower slowly recede as she continued down the street. Looking ahead, she saw four uniformed young men enter a tavern. Children then ran by, nearly knocking her down as they kicked stones to each other. By the time she regained her view of the street ahead, she had lost the vision of what could have been Ben.

Leah closed her eyes, whispering a silent prayer. She then continued forward with a hurried pace; zigzagging around a crowded marketplace, eager to lose whomever she thought might be following her.

✖✖✖✖

"Come on! I'm sure you'll bump into her again. We're starving. I bet Sal and Jacob have already been served."

For another moment Ben looked, unaware Leah had walked past. He let out a deep sigh, frustrated at the thought of having lost sight of her. He followed his brother into the tavern and found some comfort relaxing into an empty chair beside Jacob.

"Hey, what took you so long?" Sal smiled at Ben from across the table.

"Oh nothing. I thought I saw her." He sighed.

Harris took a bite out of a slab of marinated pork. He washed it down with a drink of mead. "We're here for a little longer anyways. I'm sure you'll bump into her before the next mission starts."

"Yeah, I suppose." Ben thought of months past. He had met the girl who now had a firm handhold on his heart. They shared a good-bye on the pier, exchanging gifts — a cursed medallion for a beautiful necklace. He did not want to experience that sort of good-bye again.

Sal poured Ben a jug of mead; the sound of flowing liquid retrieved Ben from his thoughts.

"So," he whispered across the table, "what do you think Nelson is going to have us do?"

Sal eyed Ben, answering with a shrug. "Not a clue. What do you think?"

"Well, it's got to be done secretly and out of the public eye."

Harris nodded in approval. "Yeah, agreed. It'd be too risky to do anything else. I mean, heck, I'm sure he'd have guards and what not, right?"

"Prime Minister. Come on, dude, that was a dumb question." Sal smiled.

They continued eating and talking about the plans of the next mission. Sal looked around at the others' partially full plates and then looked down at his to see just another mouthful of food.

"Oh my God, I've had enough. I'm tired of eating." Sal belched. He leaned back and rubbed his stomach.

"Surprised you threw in the towel this late in the game." Ben smiled.

Harris placed his utensils on the plate in front of him. "Come on now, it's the bottom of the ninth, two out, bases juiced. You're up at bat with a three and two count. Do you swing, aiming for the fences, or do you strike out looking for a fastball?"

Sal looked down at the last remnants of his meal. His friends began pounding the table in encouragement. "I … have … what … it takes!" He then shoveled down the last mouthful.

The four were laughing and smiling, enjoying the cozy atmosphere of the tavern.

Ben felt a tingling in his chest. Suddenly something wasn't right. He stood up quickly, sending his chair falling backward.

"Hey, you okay?" his brother asked, looking up from a half-eaten piece of cake.

"No, I need to get out of here right now."

"What's wrong?" Jacob gave him a comforting tap on the shoulder.

"I'm not sure. Let's just pay and get out; I have a weird feeling about something."

"Okay, the waitress just came in," Sal said as he waved her over. "Yes, can we pay our bill now?"

She smiled. "Of course, sirs, here you are."

✖✖✖

Leah walked briskly through Covent Garden, an area heralded for its street performers and entertainment. The warm feeling in her heart had begun to fade after walking for half an hour. She closed her eyes once more, trying to hone her senses and feel where Ben might be. She really did believe that they had been close earlier, but where was he now?

She sighed and stopped in her tracks, looking through the crowd of people in the bustling street. A man was juggling handkerchiefs with a group of people in a semi-circle around him cheering. A few men and women were playing lutes and other various instruments, dancing around. She decided to turn around and return the way she'd come; hoping that the last place she'd sensed Ben would be the best place to resume her search.

Leah quickly came upon Buckingham Palace. Its splendor could be seen as the sunlight reflected off of scaffolding on the northern façade. She stood at a wrought-iron gate, watching a group of workers constructing a new wing to the building. Even though she had been at the beautiful site just a day before, she smiled to herself at its pristine look, regardless of all the construction being done. Then the thoughts of her reunion with Ben the night before washed over her. Several uniformed soldiers stood at their posts, just a stone's throw from where she stood alone and in a daze. As one of the men shouldered his rifle, the sound of his buckle pressing against the wooden butt of the gun echoed in Leah's ears.

A reflection of sunlight off the soldier's rifle caught her eye. It seemed to point to the west, and she felt the urge to look where the reflection led. This mysterious feeling of following an ethereal sign caused her steps to increase with excitement. Walking through unfamiliar side streets, Leah let her feet guide her. She soon had the feeling of his presence and was frantically trying to locate it. She craned her head, stepped on her tiptoes and still could not see over the snaking flow of hats and coats that filled the cobblestone paths. Frustrated, she closed her eyes again and whispered another silent prayer. As she opened her eyes and looked around, she nearly bumped into a group of three emerging from a small and boisterous tavern.

"Excuse me." She looked up.

"Leah?" Harris looked puzzled as he stared into her eyes.

"Harris! How are you?"

"Good, just had a bite to eat with the guys." He coughed, getting the attention of his brother, who had just joined them.

Ben stared deep into her eyes, and moved through the group until he stood opposite her. He grabbed for her hand and pulled her close, his breath warm on her neck.

"I was looking for you. I sensed you. I knew you were out here somewhere," he whispered into her ear.

"I am so glad we crossed paths again. I thought I saw you earlier too so I retraced my steps, and now you're here before me."

He smiled with a newfound happiness. They stepped back from their embrace, and he allowed his friends to greet Leah properly. After the handshakes and familiarities were shared, Leah slipped a hand into Ben's.

"So, where shall we walk?" Ben asked.

She smiled, her radiance shining a path for them to follow, even as a dark shadow lingered on their trail, following in their wake through the crowded streets.

✹✹✹

*B*ack on the ship, Nelson quickly found comfort in his chair once again. He glanced up as the clock tolled the time. He smiled, flipping to the next entry, and began reading the words of Blood Bones with hungry eyes.

October 14, 1751

> *I am proving my worth to my shipmates with each battle; honing my mastery of the numerous weapons we keep aboard. I saved the captain's life in a skirmish three days ago. It was rather exciting, for I had been in the rigging with my rifle. Stationed there, I aimed at all who dared enter my barrel's sight. I had felled perhaps half a dozen men before seeing the captain cornered beside the after-mast. I had made a grave error: I had not grabbed a full powder horn before the battle. I then ran out of powder, and knowing that my rifle was now useless, I did the first thing that came to my mind; I grabbed a free line and swung through the air, letting off a blood curdling scream as my body arced downward to the wooden deck below.*
>
> *With sword in hand I landed on the deck gracefully, slicing and dicing as I stood tall and proud. I had slain my captain's attackers. Their blood was splattered on my*

face, my arms, and my legs; soaking my body to the bone. It was that day, then and there, where I earned a nickname I am now proud to carry into battle: Blood Bones.

It has a ring to it; the name roll off my tongue with ease as it makes our enemy tremble with fear. My cousin shook my hand in congratulations; I was now a formal member of the crew. Alvaro told me of his induction into the Bloods. His nickname is Blood Spot, and together we shall sail under Captain Blood Lust, wrecking havoc and disaster upon those who dare lie near.

Nelson shifted in his seat, attaining a more comfortable position, and then quickly delved back into the writings he found so interesting.

November 3, 1751

I heard a quote that has yet to leave my mind. "To reach immortality, the stories of your name must be passed on, told to all: passerby, friend, and foe. Then, and only then, you will live forever."

I have these constant dreams, of persisting through the perils of time. Not through stories or tavern tales, but through other means. I have to figure this out, I must. I know that my skills in sorcery have vastly improved since I began my nearly daily meetings with Sesostris, although I still have much to learn. From curses and spells to jinxes and hexes, I dabble with many magical elements in attempts to see what I am strongest at. Prophecies, however, interest me a great deal. He said that at our next session he would let me take a look into my future. I look forward to it.

November 4, 1751

After a day of shipboard maintenance, I met with Sesostris. From a ball of rags, he removed a crystal ball. It was clear, almost as if it was empty holding a blank future for all to see. But, my future was not blank; I had had that feeling since Captain Bernardo Bermudez had tricked me. I knew that my destiny promised more than the current situation in which I found myself.

He said in his deep and raspy voice. "Hernando, this crystal has been passed down for several generations. My ancestors before me have used this on many occasions, such as this one, to learn what is to come, and if they see something undesirable, to try to change things for the better. That is why the Egyptians were so powerful for so long. I come from an old line of Egyptian High Priests. I wish that you use this empowerment to achieve your desires and wildest dreams."

"What must happen first is for you to clear your thoughts. You must have an empty mind. Once you have accomplished this, channel your energy, your sole focus into the crystal ball."

I did as instructed. I closed my eyes, let the serenity of the vessel's rocking calm me. My hands moved on their own, massaging my temples. One stroke. Two strokes. Three strokes. My mind was clear; an empty space, just as the crystal ball had been before my eyes had closed.

"You may open your eyes. The prophecy is ready for you."

Again, I followed his instructions. As my eyelids opened, the room's light seemed to penetrate into my brain; images began to appear inside the ball. Beginning as a misty cloud, the forms began to take shape.

There were three boys, younger than myself. They

were carrying light in the form of a thin tube. They probed the darkness, as if looking for something. Through a long, downward-sloped tunnel, they proceeded. They stopped at the edge of a fast-flowing river. Jagged poles stuck out, waiting to happily impale any who had not deserved to pass over by the two parallel ropes. Next, the scene flashed to a mosaic, of a skull and bones. The black and white clashed together to make the image. They continued forward, moving to yet another room. As if they had nowhere to go, they could only move up. They climbed and at the top, a desk with a note pinned to it sat there waiting to be read. The image became clear, as if my eyes were hovering over it. I was shocked: the message was written in my penmanship.

The group continued forward, past rooms laden with treasure. But in the last cavern lay two items: a chest and what seemed to be a man. Alive or dead, I could not tell. The view changed once again, and now I could see my face, awaiting the arrival of these three adventurers with a smile. My clothes hung loosely upon fleshless bones. As they opened the chest, a light of orange and yellow brilliance radiated outward.

I fell to the deck; my face kissed the wooden planks. My pulse was heavy and my brows dripped with sweat. I had found it. My immortality now had a savior; I just have to find out how, but all that will come in due time, I suspect. Sesostris told me that prophecies come in more than one vision, in segments. I shall soon see what my future bestows, once I witness more of these alluring revelations.

Nelson's jaw dropped. After hearing of Ben and his friends' adventure on countless occasions, he began to piece the puzzle together. He inched closer to his desk, eager to read on.

13

June 22, 1763
London, England

The group was approaching the northern limits of London when they began to tire. Up ahead, they saw a stadium with a bustling crowd surrounding the locked gates.

"Ben, it feels like we've been walking forever!" Sal complained. "I need to get off my feet, I'm exhausted."

Harris nodded, prodding Jacob with an elbow to take their side. "Yeah, so are we."

Ben stood beside Leah. He felt her presence, giving him an unusual physical and emotional high. "I think I could walk for a bit more." He looked at the lass who had a strong hold on his heart. "What do you think?"

Leah bit her lip. "Well, I've always been fond of taking a nice stroll with great company, though my feet are sore from walking over all the cobblestone." She paused and then looked around, wondering if someone was still following her. "I may have rolled my ankle earlier. It would be nice to just sit down and talk."

Ben saw her anxiety and looked around also, seeing only the crowd ahead on the relatively quiet street. A sign beside the closed gate caught his eye. He began to walk closer for a better look, and as he stood several feet behind the crowd, noticing that the metallic paint on the sign said The London Cricket Club.

"I wonder why everyone is waiting," Ben said to the group.

They stood in silence, unsure of what to do or where to go. Within a minute, a large man shuffled to the locked gate from inside the stadium. He inserted a key into the lock and rotated the handle slowly. He swung it open and then stared into the crowd.

"The match will start in twenty minutes. London will play Hambledon. Tickets are five pence apiece. You may enter now. I will take your bets also upon your purchase of admission."

The man moved aside and the crowd filed in. Ben looked around and noticed the street filling up quickly.

"Let's do it!" Ben took Leah's eager hand and followed about a hundred people as the mass entanglement of bodies entered through the gate and took their seats in the rows that surrounded the playing field.

"So, what is cricket?" Jacob looked at Sal and Harris, puzzled.

"Beats me, I've never seen it played before," Harris replied.

"Any idea, Ben?" Sal looked over. "I don't think I've even heard of it."

Ben shrugged. "I've read about it once, but I have never seen a game before. It's kind of like baseball, but with a whole different look to it. I'm not really sure, to be honest."

Ben peered around and noticed the green grass of an oval field.

In the center of the playing field, there was a long rectangle called the pitch. From a distance, Ben couldn't separate the length of the grass between the pitch and the field. The crowd waited anxiously for the game to commence, and when a nearby church tolled the time, the captain from each side met with three umpires on the pitch.

"I shall flip the coin. Since London is the home team, captain, do you choose heads or tails?" the head umpire yelled to the men standing beside him.

"We will take heads," the captain of the London team said after a moment of thought.

The umpire looked to his comrades to officiate at the flipping of the coin. Once both were standing on either side of him, he flipped the coin. The sunlight shimmered off the rotating coin as it slowly made its way back to the short turf of the pitch. The coin bounced a few times and then settled. All three umpires looked down, with the captains drawing closer as well.

"Heads it is, London wins the coin toss," the head umpire called for all to hear. "Captain, do you wish to bat or bowl first?"

The captain of the London squad gave a thumbs-up to his comrades, who waited anxiously for the news. "We will bowl first." He smiled to the umpire.

"Gentlemen, please shake hands and return to your respective areas. At the sound of the whistle, London will take the field and bowl, and Hambledon will bat first. The match will consist of one inning for each team. The team with the most runs scored wins."

The captains walked to their teammates on opposite sides of the boundary, which was marked by a length of rope encircling the outer edge of the field. After a few minutes, the head umpire blew a whistle to start the match. London's eleven members took the field as two batters from Hambledon took their mark. One umpire stood on the perimeter of the field, while the head umpire stood behind the bowler's wicket, and the last umpire stood a dozen paces behind the on-strike batsman.

The first bowler stood at the ready, staring at the Hambledon batter waving the bat lightly in the air. He spit a wad of saliva into the pitch beside his feet, and then glanced into the crowd, all were eager for him to deliver the first bowl of the game. He ran a few paces forward and threw the ball overhand, aiming for the wickets beside the batter. The ball arced into the short grass and skipped back upward, spiraling toward the awaiting white willow bat. The batter sliced the ball off the side of the bat, knocking the ball off sideways at an angle.

Ben watched the batters running back and forth between the wickets, racing against their opponents in the field. The ball rolled between the fielders, almost to the boundary, and was thrown back quickly, causing the batters to stop in the creases. He heard applause from the crowd, and wondered what exactly had happened.

Harris looked at Sal in confusion. "So, what'd they do?"

Sal smiled. "Looks like the typical throw and hit if I've ever seen it before!"

Ben laughed, nudging his friend for his awful attempt at humor. "Hey guys, look at the scoreboard." He pointed to the opposite side of the stadium, where a man flipped through a collection of numbers. "The score is six to zero."

"So, that hit was worth six points?" Leah touched Ben's hand.

Ben smiled at the warmth of her touch. "I noticed the batters ran to where the other guy was and then back to his original spot. I guess that accounts for two of the six runs? I wonder if they're called runs, like in baseball?"

Harris smiled. "Sounds like it could work. You're a natural!"

"Ha! Just calling it the way I see it," Ben replied. "But I wonder where the four runs came from. Let's test my theory."

They were excited to watch the game of cricket unfold before their eyes.

The bowler hurled the ball at the same Hambledon batter, aiming for the wickets behind him. This time, the batter tipped the ball off the bat and it broke a wicket behind him.

"Howzat?" The London bowler raised a hand in excitement toward his teammates, shouting to the umpire.

The umpire replied in a loud and booming voice that carried across the stadium. "Out!"

The home crowd cheered the play, and eagerly awaited the next batter as the man who was called out walked off the field. The London bowler remained, gripping the ball slightly differently than he had in the first over. Once a new batter was ready, the bowler made a quick approach, and instead of an overhand bowl, ended up releasing at a forty-five degree angle. The ball bounced and skipped toward the batter, who swung the bat with a mighty swing.

The crowd went silent as the ball arced toward the boundary, completely clearing the grass of the outfield. Once the ball rolled to a stop, the Hambledon fans screamed in excitement as the scoreboard registered six more runs, giving Hambledon an early lead.

Ben thought for a moment, and then turned to the group awaiting his input. "Well, the batters didn't run; I guess because it cleared the boundary?"

Harris nodded in agreement. "Makes sense. So then a homerun, or whatever the term is in cricket, is worth six points?"

Ben smiled. "I guess. I mean, they got six the last time, but I think two were because of the running, so four was from hitting it toward the boundary. This last hit they didn't run between the little sticks like they did before."

Sal slapped Ben on the shoulder. "Yeah, so I guess it's four points for hits that go to the edge of the playing field, and six if it lands beyond it?"

Ben smirked. "I assume so!"

The group laughed as they figured out how the game was played. Several batters later, the score was 76-0, London still bowling to the remaining Hambledon's players. The sun was just several inches above the edge of the stadium, its glare causing Ben to shade his eyes to watch the game being played in front of him.

"Hey guys, I don't mean to spoil the fun, but I have an officers' meeting in a few hours and it will be a long walk back to the ship," Ben said to his friends.

Harris shrugged. "Boo! Don't you want to stay and watch the rest of the game? London hasn't even batted yet!"

Ben stifled a laugh. "I am sure they will come back and win. They've got the home field advantage, after all."

Leah sensed an opportunity for the two of them to be alone. As much as she enjoyed the group's company, she valued her time with Ben. "It's getting late. Would you mind if I walk back with you?"

Ben smiled. "Not at all. I could use the company."

Harris eyed Ben, hearing his response to Leah's comment. "That sounds good. We're going to stay and watch the game, so we'll meet up with you later."

"Awesome, sounds good. Let me know how the game goes!"

Harris laughed. "I thought you already said that London is going to win?"

Ben smiled. "Well, regardless. Anyways, see you guys later!"

The group shook hands, and all hugged Leah before the two figures moved through the stands. As Ben looked back to give one last wave to his friends, he noticed a figure sitting a few rows behind where they'd just been, eyeing him behind a dark cloak wrapped tightly around a body and face.

14

June 22, 1763
London, England

Ben and Leah walked through the streets in silence, observing their surroundings as well as each other, deep in thought.

"I had a fun time today with you and the guys." Ben broke the silence.

"Yes, it was nice. I enjoyed it, too." She smiled. "May I walk with you to the wharf?"

"Sure thing, but it's kind of out of your way." Ben paused. "Shouldn't I be the one to ask you if I can walk you back?"

"Nonsense; you said you have a meeting to attend and I do not have anything to do except explore the city. It's not often that we meet up anyways," Leah said. She paused for a few moments, collecting her thoughts. "I'd like to spend some time together. I've been thinking a lot about us lately."

"And what of us?" He waited anxiously, hoping for the response he had dreamt of for so long.

She paused, wanting to phrase it properly. "Well, I cannot say, for I am married and do not wish to damage the family name my father has worked so very hard for. I am just in a very unusual circumstance."

He huffed, running a hand through his hair. "Leah, what about me? What am I supposed to do? I don't think you realize that I haven't taken your necklace off since you gave it to me so many months ago. It is what kept me alive, yearning to survive all that was thrown at us. I've dreamt of you every night. I think about you every day. We need to do something about this …" he trailed off, looking at the sun slowly caressing the horizon. He became jealous of the celestial display of affection.

She seemed to follow his gaze, knowing time was running short for them, once again, as if the lack of time was the story of their lives. She pulled on his hand quickly, stopping him in his tracks. "Listen to me Ben, everything you have said I have equally done. Your medallion has yet to leave my touch, except to bathe or to remove it for a closer look. And when I lay beside my husband to sleep each night, guess who is running through my mind, holding my hand as we walk through life together. It's not Richard, it's you."

"So, is this what is to become of us, to just be there for each other in dreams and false hopes?" He began to get upset; tears slowly trickled down his cheek.

"Ben, don't get like this. We must not dwell upon these things. We are both so young. We have many years before us. Things may change in the future, but do not fret. We do not have the power to change our destiny, but only to go to where it brings us. If we end up together, I would love it just as much as you would, but for now, I do not know what to do, if there is even anything we could do."

He pulled away from her grip and began to hurry away. "That's crap. We do have the power to change our destiny! Well, I guess there's not much to do then, huh? I guess I'll just take your advice, and wait for fate to deliver me to the gallows of relationships."

"Don't get like this, Benjamin. I — come back — I have something to say," she sped up to catch him.

He slowed down and faced her, tears flowing fast as they approached the wharf.

"Fine. What is it?"

She overlooked his temperament and smiled, holding his hand gently. "I love you."

She did not wait for his response and quickly turned around, running over the cobblestones that lined the street.

A dark shadow hid behind a stack of barrels. His gaze protruded from his silhouette as the sound of Leah's footsteps echoed loudly through the alley.

✖✖✖

*B*en released a low sigh, and paced the remaining distance to the comfort of the HMS *Courtesy*.

As he stalked up the gangway, he exchanged a salute with the man on duty, who smiled. "Sir, you've a letter from the King himself, sir."

"Thank you, Mr. Roberts." Ben thought it odd for a message to be delivered so quickly after their meeting.

Too anxious to just ignore the note, Ben slipped a finger under the wax seal and with curious eyes, skimmed through the king's handwritten invitation.

A deep sigh escaped his lips as he stowed the letter in his breast pocket.

The timing of the letter was just too ironic.

✖✖✖

*C*aptain Arthur F. Nelson smiled, eager to continue reading about the exploits of Blood Bones and of his foresights of the future that included Ben and his two friends. It was ironic how their fates had been laid out centuries earlier. He opened to the next journal entry.

November 6, 1751

I had to wait a full day to recover from the prophecy, for it had drained me both physically and mentally. After thinking many hours on the topic, I realized I must discover the location of this cave. As much as I could see, there had been no hints or clues in my vision. I met with Sesostris again, and as before, he removed the crystal ball from its protective rags. I had been waiting for him to tell me to clear my head and close my eyes, but that phrase did not come.

"Look into the crystal ball. Think of the first prophecy. Continue the vision as you let yourself free flow inside the crystal."

"Yes," I said. I did as told, and then my vision changed.

There was a cellar, dimly lit, with many boxes and stacks of papers littering the area. The three familiar faces emerged into view as they began cleaning the cellar. They moved a cabinet, revealing an ancient wine rack. They pulled out each bottle, discovering a secret hidden inside of the last. A square sheet: on one side there appeared to be instructions and on the other a map. To where, I cannot say, but I itch with anticipation for the next meeting with Sesostris. Yet again, I am physically and mentally drained. The session marked another day; an unrelenting progress toward my goals of immortality and revenge.

November 13, 1751

A week has passed since my last entry. All has been well since I last put ink to paper. We've taken another small fleet: two merchantmen with three escorts. With aid from a fellow pirate captain, our two vessels eyed the horizon, seeing a lone vessel. God's breath had set their course and chose their fate, blowing them straight to our awaiting swords and shells. To say the least, we made out well.

Blood Lust mentioned a hideout near Jamaica within a few days' sail. Here our brothers of the black flag meet and trade our bounty. He says it's well protected, hidden from the eyes of our enemies. Though this excites me, my mind is solely focused on the prophecies that I've seen, and in the dreams that result.

November 19, 1751

We have been anchored inside the bay for the past few days. As my captain had described it, the meeting place is packed with several ships. I've been walking along the shore every morning since we got here. It is remarkable how this hidden sanctuary shields our whereabouts; ships sail by daily, but their scopes cannot distinguish the entrance and the hilltops disguise even our tallest mast. Here we are safe from discovery.

I would love to stay here, though the captain will likely announce a sudden departure to continue our successful raids. Perhaps someday, I can relieve del Salvado, Blood Lust, of his reign as the leader here. I see him talking with the other captains, but I've noticed he has a greater presence than the rest, being the head of the lair. I had a dream a couple of nights ago. I was standing over the bodies of those who betrayed me and made my life hell in El Morro. I had taken my justice, but it was just a dream, different from the visions I have looking into Sesostris's crystal ball. A question lingers on my lips, and tonight there is an all-hands meeting. I suppose it wise to ask my captain in private, though I may receive a degree of support if I speak my thoughts of revenge to my fellow shipmates.

I sat farthest away; the ones closest of higher rank and experience. Del Salvado took a bow, introducing himself and the crew of La Monzón, the ship that has been the only home I have known these several months. He told of our previous journeys, of the successes, of failures, and of things we could have improved on, though those were few and far between. The members of the inner circle chatted, while the outer ring sat or stood listening intently.

"Does anyone wish to add or comment?" del Salvado asked, staring at his men. I felt his eyes on me, though I could not be certain.

I stood at the cue, moving around the crowd that lined the beach. I approached the man who had given me salvation.

"I ask on my behalf. I wish to avenge my betrayers. These men do not know of my recent struggles and I would like permission to tell the tale that my lips have grown accustomed to telling."

He nodded, urging me on.

I told my story; those faces closest to me bore looks of bewilderment, as if I should not be alive. He slapped a proud hand on my shoulder. For the first time in years, it felt as if I had a father figure.

Del Salvado called out to the audience with widened hands. "My friends, what say you? Shall we give this lad a chance to fullfill his destiny? I would; he has proved his worth many a time since we have crossed paths. La Monzón is yours." He paused, his eyes seeming to stare straight into my heart. "So, who will join him on his quest?"

A wave of shock flushed through the crowd. I was an eighteen-year-old, and was just given command of a vessel? The words took a few minutes to sink in. Of course, I knew my cousin would sail with me, and along with his hand, I saw about forty more raise high to the sky.

"Unbelievable," Nelson muttered. He began a hysterical fit of laughter as he continued to shake his head at the twists and turns contained within the crimson journal.

✖✖✖

"Hello Ben, are you ready to head to the *Defence*?" Charles Marconi called out through the open cabin door.

Marconi saw his face and knew something was amiss. "Ben, are you okay?"

"Uh, yeah, I guess. I bumped into Leah." He paused. "And some other things are bothering me, but Charles, we'd better get on our way. There are more important things to focus on."

Charles thought of all the conversations he had had with his young officer, of the constant dreams Ben had of this girl named Leah. Marconi shook his head. "Ben, first comes business and then we shall talk about Leah. She is important to you; therefore she is important to me."

Ben smiled, extending a friendly hand to his friend. "I appreciate it, Charles. I brought a quill and parchment, for notes and whatever else we might need."

"Ha! You are one step ahead of me; I'll leave mine here. Well, off with us, we've a meeting to attend."

✖✖✖

In the last rays of daylight, a dark robed figure made his way down the wharf, careful to be unseen. He eyed the two uniform-clad men as they walked down the pier toward a neighboring ship. As he made progress toward the water's edge, he overheard one phrase, *the Captain's Quarters.* The cloaked figured stepped slowly into the water, making his way to the stern of the HMS *Defence.* As he lingered beside, he treaded water to stay afloat near the hull. Mumbled voices carried out from an opening in the balcony above. The distance was too great for the words to be heard clearly, so the dark figure then climbed the stern lines until he made his way to a crevice below the veranda. There, he could now hear a plan unfolding in marvelous detail.

"Good to see you again, Ben." Peter Bailey looked up from a glass of sherry.

The man stood up, placing the wine glass aside and shook hands with the two newcomers. The officers took their seats in Nelson's quarters, eager to start the discussion of the plans to come and ready to listen to what their captain had to say. Ben reached into his bag and pulled out paper, ink, and quill.

Captain Nelson cleared his throat, beginning the meeting. "Well, gentlemen, you all know why you are here. You are my most trust-worthy comrades and friends. In battles we have fought side by side. We have survived a disastrous shipwreck, and through all of these unfortunate events and hardships, we have stood together. Now is the time where our minds must unite as one, for this next mission will require a detailed plan."

All ears were open. All eyes were on Nelson. He continued. "Peter, I've been away for quite some time. For all I know, things may have changed in my absence."

"Yes, it has been quite some time, my old friend."

"So I shall pose a question," he paused. "Does George Grenville still have family in Nottinghamshire?"

Instantly, Peter understood where the question was going. "Yes!"

"I remember him mentioning a yearly ritual to hunt with his siblings, which means he will travel through, or at least, on the borders of Sherwood Forest during their expedition."

Peter nodded in agreement. "Yes, the main road does lead through those dark and dreary woods. Do you believe he will travel them?"

"Of course, he has always been senseless in that regard. Those woods are dangerous, home to bandits and common thieves. Yes, he will take this path, for it is the shortest route to their family estate north of the shire wood. A simple trap will work wonders."

Peter replied quickly. "But Arthur, how do we know for certain?"

He closed his eyes, recalling a conversation from nearly eight years earlier. His younger self walked through a crowded and well-decorated hall. He passed by ranks of officers and common militia, finally bumping into the man who would later become the country's prime minister. They had conversed for what seemed like hours, of politics, women, and family traditions.

His memory faded as the familiar faces came into view; Ben taking notes, Peter looking down into the wineglass at the remnants of sherry, and Charles and Nate engaged in a quiet conversation.

"Yes, I am certain. I would lay my life down upon those words."

"Aye, then I shall stand beside you, for you have bravely stood beside me through thick and thin." Peter smiled in return.

As the ideas and plans were passed between the two men, Ben jotted down most of what was said, but was still clearly upset from his run-in with Leah. Between jots, he would roll the quill in his fingers. Slowly, the flooding sensation of emotion overcame his eyes, and the dam broke, slowly at first and then full tilt. His tears fell onto the paper in his hands, smudging the fresh ink. He cleared his nose, but gained the attention of those who sat near.

Captain Nelson looked over, noticing Ben's clouded eyes. "Benjamin, what troubles you?"

He ran a hand across his face and then answered. "Sir, just having girl troubles," he paused, running both hands through his hair. Ben sighed deeply. "Well, Leah is married, and the king invited me to dine with Louisa Ann. The problem is my heart belongs to Leah. She just told me that she loves me."

Four heads nodded, taking in the information. "So, let me get this straight. You have two beautiful, elegant, and respectful women who are both keen on you," he paused. "Is that statement correct?"

Leah's voice was fresh in his head, her three-word phrase so clear and crisp in his mind. If only he could save it and play it over and over without having to worry over the consequences of possible actions. He was not sure if he could act upon his feelings; she belonged to a different man, but her heart was likewise trapped.

"Yes, you can say that."

"Well, here are three facts: Richard Highmore is a very powerful man. He has connections with countless officials in Parliament through his father. Leah comes from a respectable household in Grand Bahama, and Louisa Ann is cousin to King George III."

There was no sound from the audience as the words sank in.

"Aye, this is quite a situation you have there." Nelson continued. "What you should do is focus all your thoughts on you; not of the past, nor the future, but on the you of right now. Do what makes you happy. If there is a chance to run away with Leah, you must seize it, even if it means to leave us. And likewise, if you wish to sail off with Louisa Ann standing beside you at the helm, you must do so. Just do us the favor and not romance Richard Highmore; that surely would be a poor decision!"

Ben shook his head, laughing at the man's humor in even the dourest situations. "Captain, I can't leave before the mission. It's just that the timing is so piss poor with everything. She'll be going back to South Downs in a few days, and we'll be going north to Sherwood Forest. I wouldn't even know where to find her or what to do when we succeed with the mission."

"Time," Captain Nelson paused, "is always piss poor. Of that I am sure. Here's what you should do: Take a break from her. Let time tell the tale of life, as it usually does anyway. Time will be the factor; it will form and mold what could be into what is, without holding back. Fate will be your best friend, your new acquaintance for better or for worse. All we can do is wait and until then, you should take the king up on his offer. I guess my point is, you have a readily available opportunity with Louisa Ann. Do not completely give up your hopes and dreams with Leah, but rather keep them in reserve, and when applicable, drop what you are doing and seize the chance, for she has your heart, as you have hers. Don't let this slip, for you will forever dwell upon what could have been, living in your dreams for the remainder of your life. You will always regret the things you did not do."

The realization of all that had been said seemed to hang over his head, clearing his thoughts and calming his nerves. Ben smiled. "Yes, you're right as usual, sir." He cleared his throat. "I'll need liberty for tomorrow then."

Nelson nodded. "Of course, I know the guy who grants liberty." He looked down and then back to Ben. "Aye, yes, permission granted." The group billowed with laughter. "But in other news, we have a few more days to plan, and then get to Sherwood Forest before he sets out." Nelson looked at each individual before focusing on his friend. "Peter, this is where you'll come in to the plan. You must ask the prime minister to an event somewhere else." He paused, and a chuckle escaped his lips. "Just to see if he still is going to Nottinghamshire. Of course he will give an excuse, claiming he has something else more important to do. King George III says that is all he is good for — making an excuse, that is. He will apologize with a fake smile, and wish you good luck on whatever creative distraction you convey."

"That describes him well enough. So, I'll find out if he is going on the trip discreetly, then what?" Peter questioned.

"That is all, my friend; you are a neutral party in this scheme. You are a respectable figure, he will allow you entrance into his office, and you will reminisce of the glory days. Bring a bottle of wine, get some answers from him, and then we shall discover the exact day he sets out. We'll leave a day before him, make preparations in the middle of Sherwood Forest, and be back after we spring our trap. We will have accomplished this last mission and be free from duty, having all the time in the world to do as we wish."

Four heads nodded as Captain Nelson laid out the ideas. A knock on the closed door distracted their attention from planning, and a youth brought in a tray full of food.

"Here you are, sir. I sent a request for two bottles and several pipes and tobacco. The items are on the way now," the young cabin boy said.

"Most excellent," Nelson replied as the boy exited the room. "Well, let us dig in. I believe we've established a solid plan. Let us rest, drink, and be merry."

"I'll cheers to that." Peter smiled.

"Yes, that is a good plan; nay, a great plan! My throat longs for my country's ale and ciders, just as my loins long for our country's women!" Nate pounded the table, laughing jovially.

As they ate and drank in laughter, a dark silhouette of a man hidden under the balcony scurried down the stern lines, making his way slowly down the pier to report back to Captain Richard Highmore.

15

June 23, 1763
London, England

The next morning arrived excruciatingly slowly, as it normally does when you cannot stop thinking. The entire night consisted of Ben tossing and turning to the sound of the rain. Sunlight eventually filtered in through the open porthole in his cabin, and he groggily made is way to the breakfast table to join his brother and friends. All were silent as he read the king's note aloud.

> *Most loyal Benjamin Manry,*
>
> *I hope this finds you well. Please accept this invitation to my estate at Buckingham Palace. Your brave words and stories touched me, and I wish to hear more of them firsthand. We have discussed a future meeting, and it seems that this would be a most suitable time. Louisa Ann will also be present for the day's festivities, as she was also a factor in this invitation. She specifically asked for you. I shall have a carriage pick you up at the wharf at nine.*
>
> *King George III*

He looked up from the handwritten note with a shrug. "I don't know what to do, guys." He dropped his fork and knife into the dish.

Sal smiled. "Only you, Ben, only you."

"Yeah, tell me about it. Leah told me that she loves me. Why couldn't this have happened months ago?"

Jacob remained silent as usual; either off in his own little world, or just unable to open his mouth — his friends were unsure of the cause. Occasionally, however, he would speak, and when he did, it was usually something wise.

"You could always just wait for her?"

Ben looked to his left. "Wait for Leah?"

"Yes, why not?" Jacob smiled. "It seems evident that you have genuine feelings for her. Those don't come often."

Ben nodded, but before he could speak Sal interjected, "Well, her husband is old, so you could probably just wait a few more years and he'll die from natural causes — old age."

"And then move in his place, sweeping Leah off her feet, but I'd watch out for your back. You might be a little old, too, by then," Harris teased.

"Guys, I don't think that's a good choice," Ben countered. "But anyways, I guess I could just wait and see if fate works its magic."

Jacob nodded, acknowledging his comment. "Yeah, it's the best thing to do, given the circumstance."

Ben cradled a thought. "But what about Louisa Ann?"

His brother wiped his mouth with a napkin and then placed the cloth on his empty plate. "Well, it seems you are stuck between a rock and a hard place, and yet another rock. You've got Louisa Ann and Leah … and also that red-haired hooligan husband of hers to fend off. You could always hang out with Louisa Ann, though. There's nothing in the rulebooks that says you can't do that. It's not like you and Leah are married, you know what I mean?"

Ben nodded. "Yeah, I guess. You're right."

"Plus, she may even like you!" Sal added.

"I think we've already established that there, Sal. Way to be in the loop," Harris mocked.

They laughed as a sailor came to clear the dishes. From the open companionway, eight bells rung out the time. Ben had an hour before the carriage would pick him up at the wharf.

"What I meant, was that he may like her. It came out wrong, I'm sorry Mr. Serious-pants." Sal laughed.

"So you called me a girl, then?" Ben teased with a chuckle.

"Oh shush, you know what I meant," Sal said.

"Yes, unfortunately I know you too well, way too well." Ben slapped the table in mockery.

"Come on, buddy, think about it," Harris added. "Another day at Buckingham, hanging out with the king and his gorgeous cousin. Dude, if you play your cards right, you'd be set for life."

Ben looked at his brother. "Now that you put it that way, damn, what am I waiting for? I'll be on my way to my quarters to change this very second." He laughed as he stood up.

"So, are you going to wear your uniform?" Jacob asked.

He shrugged, unsure of what the customary dress would be for such an occasion. "Not a clue. I was thinking of wearing my blue suit."

"That's right, the one you got from Mr. Williamson?"

"Yeah, that's the one. It's just that I don't have anything else to wear besides my uniform. I mean I could wear some of my tarred linens, but that would be a bad idea. I should dress up at least, you know, dress to impress! The suit should be appropriate, right?"

His friends agreed with nods. The group filtered out of the mess hall, heading astern to Officer's Way. Ben opened his door with a gentle push and then looked over his shoulder. "So, uh, what are you guys doing today?"

"Eat," Sal replied quickly.

"Look at girls," Harris added.

"Watch Sal and Harris make fools of themselves." Jacob smiled.

Ben ran a hand through his hair and laughed. "Sounds like a typical and fun-filled day. I'm jealous; at least you guys aren't running through an emotional gauntlet. I feel my heart is being wrenched in two, then stepped on, then kicked, then picked up to be looked at, and lastly, dropped again to have the entire process repeat itself."

The comical expression on his brother's face dropped suddenly. Now, a serious look took over. "Bro, don't be torturing yourself over this. Think of how many people would give up their manhood for this. You've got two beautiful girls who dig you. And look at us; we still have yet to meet anyone."

Ben forced a laugh. "Yeah, I guess you're right." But inside, he still felt trapped. "Well, I'm going to change. I'll see you guys later."

"Yup, see you," his friends nodded. He closed the door quickly and another surge of emotion filled his eyes.

He stared into the mirror, looking deep into his reflection. If only he could control time, and go back to when he'd first met Leah. He drifted off into a daydream, of the two of them in the cave, the melodic sounds of waves crashing against the rock soothing their senses, setting the mood for a romantic day. For another minute he stood, transfixed in a deep, unblinking stare. With one, long exhalation; he emptied out all his amassed doubt. He reached into the closet, taking out the blue suit. He looked at it, studying the beautifully made cloth. As he began stripping off his uniform to get into the suit that would forever remind him of Leah, another deep sigh escaped his lips.

✖✖✖

*I*t was a typical day upon his prize vessel. Captain Nelson paced the deck, supervising the general maintenance aboard HMS *Defence*. Content with the safety of his crew and ship, he paced to his quarters, eager to dive into the mind of Blood Bones once more. Reaching into the drawer, he extracted the crimson journal for what he felt was the millionth time. Opening to where he'd left off, his eyes began a hurried scramble, absorbing the words written by Hernando Audaz.

November 28, 1751

> *I am writing this entry from the captain's cabin aboard La Monzón. Well, I suppose it is my cabin now.*

He moved his things out, while I brought in my few meager possessions. Del Salvado saw how bare my adornments were and then moved all his items back, telling me that it was a gift for the journey to come and a reward for my faithful service.

I am excited for my upcoming adventure, as I have conceived a plan to a high degree of detail. I see no possible failures, but as I've learned well, I have also created several backup options. Things may come up unexpectedly, but I feel that I will be blessed with good fortune, and even if things don't go exactly as planned, I won't be deterred. We leave on tomorrow's ebb for the two-day sail to El Morro.

November 29, 1751

Sesostris joins me on this next leg; as usual, he is in the mess hall. We left this morning and set course for San Juan. Del Salvado wished me farewell, good winds, and following seas. I've thought a lot about the topic of destiny, and concluded one thing: You make your own destiny.

✖✖✖

"Good morning, cousin." Louisa Ann smiled to King George III. "The sunrise was most beautiful today."

The king nodded, not entirely listening to Louisa Ann. He looked at the grandfather clock that sat opposite his desk. "Yes, yes it was. Ah, Ben should be arriving shortly." He paused. "You must be excited, I presume?"

"Of course, the prospect of a husband I may actually love would be most desirable. Though, I know I would require your approval on matters such as these."

The king nodded. "Yes, you would require my approval, and I shall grant it, for he seems a swell lad. He is young, and at such a position where he can only move up."

A voice hailed from outside of the thick doors to the king's office, followed by a short rap on the knocker.

"Yes, yes, come in."

"My king, the carriage waits at the front gate. Shall we meet your visitor at the fountain?"

"We are on our way." He looked to Louisa Ann. "You look very nice, I am certain you shall win his heart if you have not done so already."

She blushed. "Thank you, your majesty."

❊❊❊

*L*eah looked up from her morning tea, placing a book facedown on the breakfast table. The fiery head of her husband loomed just across the table, as he quickly slurped down the last bit of his coffee. He set his utensils down and then cleared his throat.

"I've some most important matters to tend to the next few days. We shall be staying in London until my … business … is finished."

She bit her lower lip, confused and puzzled. "Well, that seems most splendid. The sites are beautiful. I may walk yet again along the River Thames."

"Good, I am on my way out now. I have a very important meeting, with one of my … agents," he quickly added. "And then I will return sometime later, probably at sundown."

"Well, then, have a good day." Leah smiled, though hers was not a genuine smile of love and affection.

Captain Richard Highmore stood up quickly, eager to destroy the man who had such a firm hold on his young wife's heart, unwilling to lose her to the man introduced to him as Benjamin Manry.

❊❊❊

*N*elson stared back into the crimson journal, rereading the previous entry. He sipped at a glass of water and then wiped the moisture off his lips with a napkin. He slid back into the curves of his chair and resumed reading.

December 1, 1751

A success! My hard work, careful planning, and extreme dedication have paid off. Two of the three men who had given me great injustice have met their fate by my blade:

It was midnight; we anchored in a little inlet about a mile or so off the single road leading into El Morro. With a crew of six, we had rowed ashore. Once my feet touched soil, we rushed though the foliage and walked upon a game trail. My eyes found delight at a series of wagon tracks in the mud. We followed this path until candlelight from windows led us to the outskirts of a small town. At a corral, an old man with graying hair had his head resting back on the wall. His snores masked our footsteps, and we circled him with blades at the ready. I cleared my throat loudly, but even that was not enough to stir the man from his deep sleep. I touched the point of my blade to the man's throat, and with a slight thrust, my dear friend awoke.

"Who are you?" he said, his breath raspy and his voice old.

"I do not wish to kill you, but I will if I must," I paused. "I require a carriage. Now make haste or meet your maker."

He stared me in the eyes with evident horror; I was an eighteen-year-old pressing a blade into a man who could very well be my own grandfather. I felt a surge of disappointment flow through me at my doings, and even more so as I put ink to paper now, but the plan required this to happen, which reassured me. He did as told, for he knew I meant business. As he readied the wagon and horse, I approached him.

"Dispatch this message at sunup. Give the governor this." I slipped him a sealed letter.

He said nothing, but let out a troubled sigh.

"Remember the name Captain Blood Bones!" My whooping laugh echoed as we rode quickly down the path.

The sentry guards at the fort stopped us with pointed rifles. We relented, of course, remaining still inside the wagon. If shots were fired that early, we would have been good as dead.

"What is your business at this late hour?"

I faked a moan, my words escaping the white blanket I was wrapped in.

"What was that? Open this wagon at once!" A deep voice penetrated the canvas flap.

I moaned again, and my driver came around the carriage, placing a hand on a guard's arm. We had dressed him in the black robes of the church, and when the man in uniform turned, he repeated his question.

"One of my men has fallen gravely ill. If you wish to see him, you can, but do not expose him to the environment for too long. If you are exposed too long you will fall ill, too," he paused. "We must get him to the infirmary. Our parish lacks the proper medicinal herbs that are required to save him. He was brought to us an hour ago and has declined quickly in health. I wish you grant us access to your doctors, for with the correct medicine we may be able to save him."

The guard stood at my feet. He reached for the white blanket just at my ankles. If he had pulled it back, I am sure I might not be writing of these events. I unleashed the most blood-curdling scream I could muster, shaking violently beneath the blanket to mimic a seizure.

"Please sir, the fever is about to take over, he may only have just a few short breaths left."

His hand let loose the fabric in his grip. "Yes — do you know the way to the infirmary?"

"Of course, I have delivered many a poor soul through these very gates, bringing some to their unfortunate deaths and others to their fortunate rescue."

We were allowed to pass, and we hurried on through the familiar grounds upon which I had paced on my six-month anniversaries during what seemed so many years ago. The carriage arrived at our planned location and four pairs of hands carried my body upon a stretcher. We traveled down many stone steps on a dark spiral staircase. After a lengthy descent we arrived at a flat. Through the doorway we went, arriving at the desk of Carlos Santiago.

He looked up, startled at our approach. "Yes, what do you need?" his evil voice floated to my ears.

"We have something for you to see. My name is Father Garcia. I found a body outside of the gates. I thought he had escaped. We found him unconscious."

He sounded alarmed. "Escaped?" he laughed. "How could anyone escape from El Morro?"

"Sir, please. I wish to know if he is one of yours; if you could just identify the body."

I gripped the sword hilt that lay at my side.

"Fine, it's not like I was doing anything." He chuckled.

The sound of his laugh restored the memory of my captivity. I had waited for this moment; my revenge was just feet away. He shuffled forward.

"Move out of the way if you wish me to see the body!"

The four carriers allowed the man to stand over my body. He leaned down.

"Was he alive or dead when you found him?"

"Um, well, hard to say. He was unconscious. Perhaps, in between, barely clinging to life?"

"Ah, that's too bad. If he were to escape the dungeon, he failed to do so alive!"

The blanket was peeled off; exposing my feet first, then my thighs, my waist, and he then paused at the sound of Father Saladino approaching from behind.

"What is this, another body?" the man asked.

Two of my victims were in the same room at the same time! I smiled at the fortunate turn of events. I had expected him to be asleep at the late hour.

"He says he found the body in the courtyard." I thought I heard a shifting of robes as Father Saladino glared downward, unaware of the turn of fate that would soon happen. I waited anxiously as my face still found cover beneath the blanket.

"Well, go ahead. Reveal the face!"

A smile formed as I felt the cloth sliding across my face. My chin felt a rush of air. My nose poked out from beneath, and then my hair had fallen over my face with the last tug of the blanket.

"Go ahead, take a look." I heard from the side.

The two faces looked down at my smile, as if puzzled. I opened my eyes, feeling their stare. "Ah, Father Saladino, Carlos Santiago," I paused; their skins turned a milky white. "My name is Hernando Audaz. I was beaten and tortured by your hands. I was ill fed and treated like vermin. But, as you see, I have lived to tell the tale and have returned to this hell hole for my revenge."

Their jaws hit the stone floor.

"But, how is this possible? You fell over a hundred feet to the rocky coast. Certainly you died." Father Sala-

dino begged as if looking for an explanation. "There is no way you could have survived!"

"Well, I didn't, and I have. Remember my face in your afterlife, for my blade will send you there."

And with two quick thrusts of my blade, I now have only one act of vengeance remaining. Before leaving the room, I leaned down, and retrieved my mother's necklace from around the Father's neck.

My crew and I paced up the spiral staircase, and as we exited, soon came to discover a squad of men patrolling the yards. I had a feeling that the corral owner had disregarded my orders and had relayed my message immediately after our departure. I was not prepared to stop for them now, not when I was so close to achieving redemption.

I led my men through the courtyard, staying low and along the walls. Through the dark shadows we evaded our enemies until one group discovered us. We got to the soldiers before their rifles could be raised.

We then crossed paths with a new patrol, and were not as lucky as before. They had managed to fell one of my comrades with a rifle shot. We had to hurry now. As we passed our abandoned carriage, we saw it had been flipped over and thoroughly searched while we were deep in the dungeons. The sight inspired me and pushed me forward, giving me that extra drive to escape from El Morro for the second time.

Nelson looked up from the crimson journal in time to hear the sound of someone knocking on his door.

❈❈❈

The carriage came to an abrupt halt, causing Ben to stir from his doze. The light pitter-patter of a steady rain gave way to a cloudy sky, and he'd fallen asleep the moment he left the wharf, still exhausted from his sleepless night. He shook his head, clearing all the thoughts that continued to circulate inside. A narrow ray of light filtered in through the small window on the door until the carriage driver opened it, allowing for the inside compartment to brighten fully. Ben stood up, his blue suit contrasting with the maroon interior.

Ben made his way out of the carriage and smiled at the carriage driver and bid him farewell. As he turned, he faced King George III and the beautiful Louisa Ann, standing against a background of the octagonal water fountain spewing water at all angles. The sight was magnificent. He smiled as he closed the distance to the awaiting figures.

"Good morning, my king." He bowed. "And to you, Lady Louisa Ann." He took her outstretched hand, and pressed his lips to her white gloves.

"Welcome to my home yet again," the king said.

"I have never seen a place such as this." Ben spoke with honest words.

The monarch clapped Ben a proud pat on the shoulder. "There is much to talk about, Benjamin. You have stories I wish to hear, and for that, we must make our way inside."

"Yes, I am looking forward to it."

The group made their way up the entrance staircase into Buckingham Palace.

"Are you hungry?" The king looked over his shoulder.

"I had a light breakfast before I left," Ben said.

"I see. Well, let us go to my favorite room, the observatory and study. If you wish to have something to eat, I shall get my servants to prepare whatever it is you desire. But until then, I shall ask you to follow my lead."

Louisa Ann followed in their wake, falling slowly behind. Ben felt the warmth she radiated fading and he slowed down.

"Why thank you, kind sir." She smiled.

He felt that he had passed the test. Ben's head lowered a few inches and with a slight nod. "Of course, a woman such as you should not walk alone."

The king continued his pace as Ben and Louisa Ann distanced themselves.

"You look handsome in that suit."

He smiled, his mind full of thoughts of standing inside Mr. Williamson's closet, picking out the striking suit so many months ago. He took a moment to clear the thought before speaking. "Thank you. It usually takes me a while to look presentable. I mean, you, on the other hand — I am sure you could fall into a puddle of mud and still look better than all the remaining women in London."

The words seemed to slip out of his mouth, with no explanation as to why he said them. The advice his friends and fellow officers had given him earlier seemed readily at hand. He had her at a loss for words. She blushed.

She paused, responding with a return of equal stature. "Well, Benjamin. It rains often here in London, as I'm sure you've realized. So, for me to fall into a puddle and stand a beauty as you say, it could be quite possible." Her response was so unnatural and forced that she could not help but giggle.

Ben smiled, shaking his head. "Ah, it seems you cannot compete with my witty tongue." He laughed, playing the flirting role perfectly.

"In due time, Benjamin, in due time I wish to compete." They continued their private walk as they began to catch up with the king.

George looked back, seeing that they had fallen behind. He smiled with satisfaction; it seemed as if all had fallen into place. Ben and Louisa Ann had taken to each other, as he had hoped.

"Now, it is just up this stairwell," he announced. His hand found the doorknob, and he gently shoved the door open. There was no creaking of the hinges, for this was the most used path in all of Buckingham Palace. "We shall ascend to the heavens, or, well, at least very near."

He began the climb, the spiral staircase continuing up and up for as long as the eye could see. They at last came to a flat entrance decorated by several paintings and golden mirrors.

"Ah, we are here," King George III said as he stepped through an open doorway.

The room was massive.

An enormous globe caught his eye. It measured over four feet in diameter from South to North Pole. The gold globe shone brightly, tinkling as candles overhead flickered from the open window.

The rain continued to fall, but it was now more of a mist than anything else. It brought in a fresh smell, giving the air a tasteful treat of something other than the odor that came from the mountains of old leather volumes and heaps of Oriental carpets and rugs around them. Ben looked around, trying to count the total number of books on each shelf. He gave up after one row, stupefied at the personal library that the king possessed. The man's wealth was beyond comprehension.

"This is amazing."

The king smiled at the young officer who stood befuddled before him. His laugh echoed off each placard. Lustrous paintings seemed to vibrate, too, as if applauding the collection that filled the vast space. Metal suits of armor stood lining a far wall with weapons slanted at the ready to fend off an attacking enemy. Before the open window, Ben studied a large telescope.

"Wow, I've always wanted a place like this to write and think," he said, taken aback by the room's magnificent aura.

"On clear nights, I can see all that the heavens have to offer, all its beauties, everything — stars, planets, distant twinkles of light. For hours, I will sit on that very chair and just stare off into space. Yes, I am the leader of a country, of countless people, but yet at the same time, I am just one. It clears my head. The beauty of it all just boggles my mind."

Ben pressed his brow to the eyepiece, adjusting the zoom to from its previous setting. The scope was aimed into the heavens, and he stared up into a dense and dark cloud overhead. Through holes in the cloud, he could see a patch of blue of sky beyond. A strong wind picked up, shaking the leaves on the trees that lined the perimeter of the estate. The clouds cleared as the sun shone brightly, and the last drops of the steady rain fell, changing it into a sunny day.

"It seems it will be a pleasant night for star gazing," the king announced as he peered through the window.

"I agree. It has turned into a lovely day. Though I could spend an eternity inside this room."

"Well, then. Let me have some food brought up." His majesty laughed. "You'll need some energy if you wish to stay up here forever."

The king moved to a writing desk. Atop the oak table sat a golden bell. He rang it for a few seconds and then waited. Moments later, a middle-aged woman entered the room.

"Good morning, your majesty." She curtsied.

"Same to you, Martha. Bring up a tray of tea and the usual delicacies."

"Yes, my king."

The servant exited, leaving the room in silence. Louisa Ann stood to the side, at a loss for words. Her eyes were half closed. Ben felt her gaze and he acknowledged it with a smile. She blushed once more.

A group of servers entered carrying trays of cups, silverware, and freshly baked raisin scones.

They were set on a table and the servers left as quickly as they had come.

"Ah, my favorite; fruit scones, I wonder what flavor it is today." The king moved to the silver tray.

He looked down, releasing a pleasant sigh. "Most excellent, raisin!"

Ben and Louisa Ann joined George at the table. After each took a cup of steaming tea and a dish piled high with scones, the king led them to a corner of the room. The sitting area had enough space for a small party, and they each took a seat in the comfort of the leather couches.

"So, Benjamin, tell us one of your stories."

Ben looked at the king, unsure of what to say. He paused, and then something made him smile. "Knock-knock."

They sat dumfounded.

"Say, *Who's there?*" He smiled.

Louisa Ann replied a split second before her cousin. The combination of voices clashed.

"Interrupting cow," Ben answered. They sat there, still awaiting further instructions.

"Say, *Interrupting cow who?*"

As their lips began to form the words, Ben cried out a loud moo. The king dropped his saucer in a fit of laughter. Louisa Ann smiled, her body vibrating with amusement.

"Okay, well, I guess the eighteenth century isn't totally ready for knock-knock jokes," he whispered. "Perhaps I can share a story that you will never forget?"

His audience nodded with excitement. Ben began his story, the familiar tale spiraling into life, as they were eager to grasp every detail of his experiences since joining up with the crew of the ill-fated *Frendrich*. Of course, it was necessary to omit several factors.

✖✖✖

Nelson looked up from the journal that lay sprawled before him. His eyes gazed at the now opened door. A messenger stood there, a note held tightly in his hand.

"Sir, a note from a Mr. Peter Bailey." He stood waiting instruction.

"Yes, bring it here please," Nelson replied.

The messenger moved closer, stopping before the desk. His outstretched hand placed the note into Nelson's hands.

"If you will wait outside until I call you."

"Yes, sir." He touched his brim in salute and about-faced, leaving the quarters in silence.

With nimble fingers, the captain opened the message. Staring at the smudges of ink, he realized just how fresh the information was.

Arthur,

> *We do have not much time to act on our plans. He will be leaving his estate for the northern woods in two days. I hope you have readied all that needs readying, for we must leave with the sunrise on the morrow to achieve all that we have discussed. Do not worry about a reply; I will be at the foot of your vessel by noon. I have dispatched a similar message to the king.*
>> *Until we meet next,*
>>> *Peter*

Nelson placed the feather inside the fold of the crimson journal; marking his place for the next time he had time to read. He sighed, hoping the mission would go as planned.

✖✖✖✖

Jacob fell behind, and Harris and Sal took the lead on their latest excursion through the city of London. He paused to tie his shoes, but when he looked up he had lost sight of his friends. Quickening his pace, he maneuvered through a group of children. A cart of fresh baked bread rolled out into his path, emerging from a side street. He bounded to the side, nearly knocking down a young blonde girl.

He stared into Leah's familiar face.

She smiled. "Hello, Jacob. It seems that we bump into each other quite frequently on these streets."

He laughed, his eyes still surveying the streets for his missing comrades.

She noticed his distraction. "It seems you are looking for someone, or something?"

"Oh yes, I bent down to tie my shoes, and then lost sight of Harris and Sal," Jacob replied.

"No Benjamin?" she asked, a puzzled look growing on her face. "I always see the four of you together."

The conversation over breakfast circulated fresh in his mind. Jacob was slow to answer, but he could not tell Leah a lie; it would be wrong to do so. "Well, he is actually with Lady Louisa Ann and King George III at Buckingham Palace. They requested him to spend the day."

Leah's heart sank. She stopped walking, realizing that there was someone else in his life, even though she was in a similar situation. She instantly became jealous, and warm tears began forming in her eyes.

They stood in the center of the crowded cobbled street; buggies passed by quickly, children ran at their feet playing, and there were vendors selling their wares. Their silence was interrupted by the arrival of Harris and Sal.

"Hey man, we thought we lost you!" Harris smiled. From his view, he only saw Leah's golden locks.

Leah turned around upon hearing his voice, and Harris quickly paled.

"So, Benjamin is off gallivanting with her?" Her eyes stared right through Harris.

He was shocked by her bluntness. He could only nod.

Harris then shot a quick look at Jacob, but returned his gaze to the teary-eyed girl who stood before him. "Listen, I'm sorry. I don't know what to tell you. Ben is a good kid; he wouldn't go out of his way to hurt you. He's not like that."

"Well, tell him he did — and that I wish to never see him ever again."

Her words were thrown out quickly and carelessly, fueled by her hurt, but at that specific moment in time, she meant every word she said. Leah turned on a heel and rushed off through the crowd, not looking back once.

16

June 23, 1763
London, England

The king stretched, yawning deeply. "Your stories have passed two hours of our time! I am afraid my legs have grown sore. I need to get up and stretch."

Ben smiled. "I hope I have not bored you."

"Oh, Benjamin, of course not! To hear this story from your very own lips is of such great interest. I have read these accounts in print, but it is nothing in comparison to sitting across from the man who fought Blood Bones, Blood Spot, and Mad Dog. Those three villains were the cause of countless headaches. I still do not know how to fully repay you."

He smiled. His eyes were drawn to Louisa Ann; her beautiful dark hair was pulled back into a loose bun. One lock seemed to fall over her left eye; she kept moving the stray hairs to sneak stares at the young man who sat just a few feet away. Their eyes caught, and both of them blushed.

The king noticed this, but did not verbalize his approval. "Well, shall we proceed outdoors for the time being?"

"Yes, that is a good idea, cousin. I would like to ride for a bit," she paused. "Ben, I do not believe I told you this, but I ride horses for sport. I have won many races and events the past few years."

"No you didn't, but if we race, be prepared to lose," he said with a playful wink.

She cheerfully giggled, placing her teacup aside. "My king, would you mind if we excuse ourselves and ride around the estate for a little while?"

"Not at all, dear Louisa Ann. It is a swell day for it, though the grounds may still be wet. I will take a stroll myself," he paused, taking sight of the clock. "It is quarter until noon; let us meet beside the grand fountain at one."

Two heads bobbed as she stood up, grabbing hands with Ben and towing him out of the room. The king stood slowly, making his way to the open windowsill. He sighed with contentment; happy the day was going as they had both hoped. Moments later, two figures emerged into view below, holding hands and running excitedly toward the stables just a stone's throw away from the main building.

A knock on the door behind caused him to look back as a messenger entered the quiet study.

"Your majesty, a message from Mr. Peter Bailey."

King George III smiled at the man's name and remembered his association with Arthur F. Nelson.

"Good, good. Let me see." His hand extended toward the note.

"Yes sir. He said there is no need to respond." The messenger bowed and left as quickly as he had come.

George returned to the window and glanced quickly from the written update back to Ben and Louisa Ann, enjoying each other's company.

"Ah, lovely," the king whispered to the window.

✖.✖.✖

"Have you ever ridden before?" Louisa Ann asked.

Ben craned his head in thought, the individual occurrences fresh in his mind. "I can count the amount of times on a single hand. I am still learning, I suppose, but I don't let my inexperience stop me from attaining victory," he said with a wink.

She looked at Ben. "Well, you are in luck, for I am a great teacher. Oh, I should change into my riding gear. Do you have an extra set of clothing?"

He shook his head. "No, I'm fine. I'll just wear this."

Her lips parted, showing a smile full of white teeth. "Okay then, I will return shortly."

He nodded, watching Louisa Ann leave. For the past few hours, he'd barely thought of Leah. It was as if she did not exist. His stare into space continued, and before he knew it Louisa Ann gave him a gentle nudge upon her arrival.

"Are you okay?" She stood before him.

He realized that he'd drifted off, and smiled. "Yes, I do that frequently, I'm sorry." He grabbed the rein of the horse that a stable hand brought forth and followed Louisa Ann and her own horse out of the stable.

"Not a worry." She led her horse down a well-groomed path and headed toward a wooded area.

There were several minutes of silence between them as the two made their way to the wood's edge. Off in the distance there was an equestrian course. Ben looked out, unsure of what to expect.

"You look puzzled." She smiled. "We walk the horses here." She pointed, looking down into a rough circular path. "You can see the hoof prints."

He stared down, seeing depressions in the wet earth. "How long do we walk the horses before we can ride?" he questioned.

"I ride them every day, so they only need about ten minutes of walking, and then a gentle trot before we do the course."

Ben nodded, learning something new with every step forward. He gripped the reins loosely in his hand and followed Louisa Ann. They walked for a few circles in silence, enjoying the sun's warming rays on their grinning faces. He looked around, seeing the evaporating mist upon the grand lawns of the king's estate.

"I believe we have walked them enough," she paused, looking up into Ben's blue eyes. "We can get on, and then trot along this field." She pointed, tracing out the next phase of the intricate warm-up.

"Okay," he said as he followed suit, stepping up into a stirrup and swinging a leg over.

Louisa Ann led the way, looking back every so often to see how Ben fared. "It took me a few months to get comfortable. I am sure you will do fine."

They followed the path along the woods, and then turned to follow a small brick wall. They did the course twice. "Okay, are you ready?" she called over her shoulder.

"Let's do it!" He took a firmer grip on the reins, eager to feel the difference between the slow trot and a gallop.

Ben watched the horse beneath Louisa Ann's small frame kick up several small stones as it propelled forward. His horse seemed to follow without instruction; he kicked his feet into the horse's ribcage, feeling like John Wayne.

"Yah! Yah!" He egged the horse on. "Come on, boy!"

Louisa Ann remained a constant length in front, but as the horse below him increased speed, his whole body bounced up and down violently. The saddle wedged into his thighs and groin, causing grunts of pain to escape his mouth with every step.

She looked back to see his grimacing face. She grinned. "It helps if you stand in the stirrups."

He adjusted his weight again, placing nearly all of it in the stirrups. From this position, he could now ride with ease. He smiled, feeling new. The wind whipped against his face, blowing his hair back. If only he had a cowboy hat and a lasso or a Smith and Wesson slung on his hip, he would be straight out of a movie.

"Yee haw!" He held an imaginary brim, waving the invisible hat to and fro.

Louisa Ann looked back again, and her laugh carried to his ears. He was having the time of his life. She was so much fun, so beautiful, and most importantly, single. The last word stung his heart. The thought of Leah being married infuriated him. Ben despised Richard Highmore for taking his love away from him. He was absorbed in the daydream, unaware that Louisa Ann had just jumped a hedge. The horse below him arced upward following behind, its hooves clearing the green foliage below. All of Ben's weight was back, not leaning into the jump like it should have been if he had been paying attention.

The momentum forced him to reel backward, falling off the horse into a puddle of mud. His right foot slid out of the stirrup but his left remained twisted in. The horse continued to follow Louisa Ann. Time seemed to slow as his body bounced off the ground below, dragged by his mount. She looked back to see his progress, until that moment unaware of the mishap.

"Benjamin!" She reeled her horse around. "Het, het!" she clicked her tongue loudly and the oncoming horse responded.

The horse towing Ben stopped suddenly, causing him to crash into its powerful legs. He moaned in pain, the shock of what had just happened ceasing all other movement. Louisa Ann slipped off her saddle quickly, moving to Ben's side. She placed a hand on his leg, moving it slowly to see if anything was broken. She twisted the caught stirrup and freed his foot.

"Are you okay?" She looked down with caring eyes.

He blinked several times, his face covered with dust and mud, with speckles of blood strewn in the mix. The sun brightened, casting a shadow around the figure that loomed above. Slowly, sense and movement came back to him. She helped him sit up carefully. The pain in his back, neck, and foot throbbed.

"What happened?" he asked in a whisper.

"You took a bad fall. Your foot got caught and the horse dragged you." She looked down at the cuts and abrasions on his face, as well as the ripped blue suit.

She lent a hand to help him stand. Putting his weight to the ground, he pushed against the moist grass and regained his feet. He stood there for a moment, still dazed from the fall.

"We must get you inside." She guided him slowly across the large lawn. She turned, clicking her tongue for the horses to follow. The beautiful animals obeyed the command.

✖.✖.✖

The king's personal physician stood over Ben's bare body. A towel had been placed over him for modesty, as he lay motionless on the observation table. Beside sat a bowl of bloodied water and a red-stained towel. A long gash ran along his left ribcage, still bleeding, and the doctor's hand pressed firmly against him with another cloth to stem the bleeding.

Louisa Ann stood beside King George III, her hands crossed. Her cousin remained silent; watching the physician clean Ben's numerous wounds. She continued to stare at Ben's athletic body. Minutes ticked away slowly on the clock that sat on the mantelpiece above the fireplace. After an hour, the doctor turned around.

"He will be fine, just many abrasions and bruises all over his body. He is extremely lucky to not have died, or even broken something. To be honest, I was surprised to find him conscious. Rest is what he really needs."

The king nodded, extending a hand. "Doctor, our thanks again."

The man wiped down all his instruments with a clean white towel and then stowed his equipment in a black leather bag.

He looked down at the patient. "Benjamin, just clean the wound once a day with fresh water and a towel. I have bandaged it now; you should change it after a day."

"Thank you, sir." Ben managed with pain.

The doctor left the room. Pausing at the door, he looked over his shoulder. "Enjoy the rest of the day." He touched the brim of his cap and pushed through the door.

The king motioned for a servant to enter. The elderly woman moved slowly across the room.

"Go to my chambers; get him a new suit, shoes, and some fresh undergarments."

"Yes, my king." She turned and left the room.

"Well," the king said, "let us get you back to the ship. You need the rest, and I'm sure you've some business to tend to."

Ben caught the glimmer in the king's eye and roused himself. It seemed as if he knew something Ben did not. "Yes, sir, I'm sorry we couldn't have spent more time together." His eyes drifted slowly toward Louisa Ann. "I had a great time today, even though I still can't feel half my body." Ben smiled at his clumsiness.

"As did I. Would you like to do this again?" She stared at the servant who carried in a gray wool suit for Ben to change into.

"Yes, I would. Everything except falling off the horse." He smiled. "But even then, it was still a great day." They left him a moment so that he could change. Stiffly, he managed to get into the new clothing, careful not to shift the bandage so that blood might ruin the new jacket. When he was dressed, he found them near the entrance hall. He lifted an aching arm to salute the king, turned toward Louisa Ann.

She offered her hand. Ben bowed to press his lips against her gloved hand. He looked out, past the gate to the awaiting carriage. Turning his head, he touched a hand to his forehead. "Sir, have a great day. Thanks again for the invitation."

"It is an honor to be in your presence, my young friend." The king extended a hand. He gestured to the bundle Ben held. "Do you wish to leave your soiled suit here to be discarded or washed?"

Ben shook his head firmly. "No, thank you, sir. I'll bring it back to the ship," he paused, thinking Leah and the in-between uncertainties of the situation.

A sentry snapped off a salute as he passed through the gate. The carriage door was opened for him and he stepped inside. Peering through the iron bars of the gate, Louisa Ann smiled. She waved as the carriage propelled forward, heading through the bustling streets of London.

❊❊❊

Leah sat hunched beside a tree crying into her hands. Sniffling, she wiped the free flowing tears from her eyes. Her gaze scanned the horizon; from her perch on a hillside above the wharfs, she could see two British ships alongside the pier. She did not have to see their nameplates, but she knew which vessels they were: HMS *Courtesy* and HMS *Defence* rested easily in their berths. A lone figure in a gray suit walked the length of the pier, with a bundle of blue clothing in his arms. He walked with a limp, a slow and deliberate step. For several minutes she watched the young man from afar.

His medium-length dark hair was parted in the middle. His white skin seemed to reflect the last rays of light as the sun danced on the horizon, sinking slowly to the blue line between water and sky in the distance. He moved to a bollard, sitting atop the metal structure. Ben sat for a long while, his gaze off into the water, pondering just as Leah was. Her heart pumped harder, beating against her ribcage. She knew it was Ben, but there was not much she could do. They were far apart, and by the time she found a way down the hillside to the pier to confront him it would likely be too late. What would she even say to him? She sighed deeply, observing the young man who had stolen her heart, stifling a cry, as Ben was still the only man she truly loved.

Finally, he stood up. He crumpled the blue suit into a ball, and walked a few feet to the water's edge. He hurled the blue cloth into the ebb tide, the waters slowly tumbling the bundle out to sea. Ben sighed, his internal struggle leaving with the deep exhalation.

Her tears flowed with renewed temper, watching the display with clouded eyes. As Ben turned around, he felt as if he was being watched. He stared out onto the wharf, searching between piles of cargo from neighboring ships. For several minutes he scanned the length of the pier. He finally gave up the hunt, lowered his head, and limped up the gangway of his vessel to the comfort of his cabin.

17

June 23, 1763
London, England

Ben stood in front of the door to his cabin, studying a pinned note. His body ached from the earlier incident; all he wanted to do was lay down. With nimble fingers, he slid open the waxed seal. His eyes darted across the message.

Benjamin,

Come to my quarters as soon as you get this. I've news to share regarding our upcoming plans.

Captain Arthur F. Nelson

✖✖✖

Ben's knuckles wrapped hard upon the door. A voice from inside told him to come in. Gripping the handle, he pushed through, entering a crowded room. All eyes looked at Ben as he limped into their view.

"Are you all right?" Nelson called from behind his desk.

His face grimaced with pain as he took a seat between the first and second officers. He made eye contact with everybody in the room.

"Yes, sir. Just took a nasty fall off a horse. I just need to rest a bit," he replied.

"Well rest up as much as you can before we leave," Nelson said. "The day with Lady Louisa Ann otherwise went well?"

He nodded. "Yeah, she's a great girl. I think I'll forget about Leah for the time being; it just hurts too much to know she's with someone else and not with me, regardless of how she feels."

Nelson's head bobbed up and down. "Yes, we've all been there at some point in our lives. But men, I have pressing issues to discuss with you all." He turned to the others. "Peter brought to me information of the Prime Minister's movement. He will ride north in two days. This means we will leave tomorrow at sunup, ride to Sherwood Forest, and set our trap."

His men listened attentively, mentally preparing for what was to come. Their talk lasted long into the night. One by one, his officers left, leaving Ben the last in the small room.

"Before you leave, I'd like for us to talk for a moment," Nelson said, gesturing for Ben to retake his seat. "I have a few more pages to read in this crimson journal. Blood Bones was quite the character. The things he did as a young man are quite astonishing. He was your age when he escaped from *El Morro*, diving a hundred feet into the waters below. It is truly remarkable that he survived the fall."

Ben pictured a figure leaping from the thick, protective walls of a huge fortress. In his mind he could see the large smile of Blood Bones as he waved to him, descending into an unknown fate that lingered below. It was a similar fate, of crossed-paths.

"So," Nelson paused, waiting for Ben to regain his senses. "From what I observe, you have donned a new wardrobe since departing earlier."

"Yes, well, as I said before, I fell off a horse. We were riding a course, and she took the lead and I followed. I wasn't paying attention, as I was about to make a jump. I didn't lean into the jump and

I rolled off backward. My foot got stuck in the stirrup and I got dragged for a little."

The captain shook his head, a smile forming on his lips. "Ah, seems like you should get some riding lessons after this next mission."

Ben laughed, stretching a few kinks out of his neck and back. "Other than that, it went really well. For the first time, I think I can get by without having Leah plague my thoughts. I even threw away the blue suit her father gave me."

The captain's smile dropped quickly. "Why would you do that?"

He remained silent. "Well, it was shredded from the fall and being dragged by the horse, but … I don't know. I sat on the pier for a while, just thinking everything over. I mulled over it for awhile and I didn't know what else to do."

"I suppose. Memories are best lived as memories. Sometimes physical remembrances are often too difficult to bear. I would keep just one thing to remember her by, as to not completely rid you of her. She has influenced your growth as a man, regardless of whether you are aware of that. Keep her locket close to your chest, but do not let the memories destroy you from within. You are young, very successful, on yet another adventure that you will be telling your grandchildren when that time arises."

"You sure do speak well," Ben replied. "I should write all your little speeches and quotes down and make a book out of it, *Motivational Words by Captain Arthur F. Nelson*," he recited, letting his words take effect. "It sure does have a nice sound to it!"

The captain laughed, slapping his thigh with an open hand. "You have developed so well in the past several months. You have become a grand officer and also a gentleman that women around the world will always desire!"

"Thank you, sir. I couldn't have done it without you; you have helped a lot, especially as of late. It's just really tough to desire something so much, and when it's almost within reach, your fingertips graze it, but you can never actually get a solid handhold upon it."

"That, my young friend, is how life works. What comes easy is not always the most desirable thing. Sometimes you have to suffer through pain, tragedy, and misfortunes, to attain the desirable. If you skip the process, it really wasn't worth it!"

"I'd love to sit and chat; I could easily spend the night here telling you what I am thinking."

"As could I, but we have much to do tomorrow and the day next. Anyways, how do you feel?" He eyed a slight wrinkle of pain in the corner of Ben's mouth as he shifted uncomfortably in his seat.

He shrugged. "Nothing as bad as the encounter in Grand Bahama." Again his mind drifted off, thinking of the night he had met Leah, and of the injuries he sustained while protecting Leah and her mother from the drunkards. For several moments he sat motionless, staring into space as he thought of what could have been. Slowly, the images receded into the corners of his mind. "Well, I've suffered worse; I just need a night's rest. I'll see you on the pier at six."

"Yes, get some rest. Our ride should take most of the day."

He watched Ben stand slowly and bid him good night. As the young third officer exited the room, Nelson once again opened the crimson journal that sat atop his desk. His fingers traced through the previous entry and finally he dove back into the mind of Blood Bones.

December 2, 1751

> *We rowed back to La Monzón immediately upon our return to the inlet. Greeted by my crew, I relayed my story.*
>
> *"Three cheers for Captain Blood Bones!"*
>
> *My men were jolly that evening with song and drink, and their merry voices floated to my cabin as I basked in the glory of my success. Moonlight spilled in through the balcony window, and I smiled as Sesostris entered into my quarters.*
>
> *The empty crystal ball stared me in the face. I smiled,*

touching its base as always, and then channeled my thoughts, dreams, and wishes into the void spaces of its mysterious powers. Clouds of images appeared, taking form in the time that passed. A hand passed quickly across my view; a scarlet ring flashing bright. But where had I seen that before? It looked familiar, as if my own hands had touched it many times in my dealings with Captain Bernardo Bermudez. The connection dawned on me, and I inched my face closer to the crystal ball. The hand then opened a crimson journal with gold inlaid into the cover. Ripping out a page, the hand began to draw out a map. The hand flipped the sheet over, but failed to put ink to paper. The image then faded as all my energy flowed outward.

I moaned with pain; exhaustion filled my body. So now I knew two things: that I had ripped out a page from my, well this, journal, and that I was the one who had created the map that would eventually lead the three young adventurers to find my treasure. This constant, yet ever-growing mystery is alluring, completely encompassing every second of every minute of every hour in which I dwell. If Poseidon is kind to me, he will push La Monzón with a blissful breath to my next destination.

My next entry will not be until I meet again with Sesostris, for there is no need to write when I am not currently seeking merchant vessels for plunder. It is not a high priority at this time in my life. Imagine, Captain Blood Bones, saying that I do not wish to expand my purse with the riches of foreign spoils? However, my reputation grows, I suppose if my message to the governor of San Juan has been delivered, which I believe it to have been done, and then I am most certain they have found the two bodies in the dungeons. Perhaps they will link me, Hernando Audaz, to the killings. I think not; I was nobody back in my early years, and I am sure that no one ever remembers me from my youth. But now I am some-body: a fearless pirate — Captain Blood Bones.

December 16, 1751

It's been two weeks since we set sail for Barcelona, and several times I have met with Sesostris. To no avail, the crystal ball shows no further prophecies, just revisions of previous images of the ring and journal for the most part. I feel that these two objects must be important, so important in my quest for immortality, as well as in my plans for redemption. My noon fix shows us roughly half-way across the Atlantic on our northeasterly course.

With each day that passes, I feel I come closer to find-ing Bernardo Bermudez. Sesostris says that the reason for my lack of vision is because I require the ring; I need it like I need oxygen. I need it like I need revenge. To have eternal life, I must wear this ring. On its own, the ring will not keep me from death, but I must have these important items. This journal that I write in must be one of those items as well. Are there more? There must be, only two items seem improbable. The spoken words I heard so many nights ago in my Commanding Officer's quarters, of a treasure in the holds of El Morro — Wait, that is it. El Morro is involved too, and I was just there, sitting atop the bounty of Sir Francis Drake. The treasure must wait until I am finished. I have another life to take before I can search for the last puzzle piece.

December 28, 1751

We have arrived in my homeport of Barcelona three days after Christmas. The festivals continue on; crowded streets and music constantly fill the air with a joy that brings memories back of my childhood. I have sent out many invitations; among them one to Bernardo Bermudez, and the other to men I accompanied to San Juan so long ago. Their names would forever be etched in my mind, so with ease, I learned of their whereabouts and tracked them down. One by one, I had spied them and delivered my letters.

I knew of a perfect location to carry out the plan, so I rented out a ballroom at quite a burden to my purse, the cost of which is of no real importance, for that will be the next phase of my elaborate plan. I must wait another three days before I act, and then after, we set sail for El Morro.

December 31, 1751

I am about to leave for the ballroom, but have paused to put my thoughts to this crimson colored journal once more. I feel that it is becoming a part of me. Perhaps my immortality is just a figure of speech, as the saying goes: through my stories and tales. We shall soon see, but as I ready myself for the masquerade, I continue to beam a smile that is of pure happiness.

January 1, 1752

A new year brings exciting news; all my sleepless nights of planning have proven worthwhile.

As my guests entered dressed in their array of costumes, I hid in the shadows, watching for the faces I had dreamed of for so long. My crew was dressed in white, disguised as servers. When my fifty guests had been seated, I *made sure to linger in hiding for just a minute longer. On cue, music played from the center of the ballroom stage.*

A gentle mix of sound filled the beautiful hall. Tables were set with the finest imports. Masks sat in the laps of suits and gowns. I had made sure to not only invite my special guests, but also many names of those serving in Parliament, at the High Council, and in other well-known areas of society. They had to witness my plan unfold, and unfold it did!

Placing my mask over my face, I walked in with a slow gait to stand before the conductor. I turned my back to my audience, hiding a last minute smile. I raised my arms up high, cleared my throat, and said the name that had been etched into each hand-made invitation.

"Francois Drake."

I had to do it; I'd had to disguise my identity, for there was a chance that they might recognize my real name, even if the chance was slim to none. Why that name? I don't really know. Perhaps because of the connections that the English Privateer has to my story, but honestly it was the first name that came to mind when I crafted my plan of revenge. I stared into the crowd from behind my red mask. My eyes filtered through unknown faces, my gaze stopping on those who had betrayed me.

"That is the name to which I find my body attached." I continued. "My soul longs for things that most deem desirable, though I shall let you in on a grand secret." I paused, leaning forward as if to whisper. "I hope you enjoy the food, music, and dance to celebrate the end of a year and the beginning of another. It seems to me a cycle of life, death, and rebirth. Giovanni, please play a tune as the servers bring in the first course."

The music began as the doors from the kitchen opened.

I heard whispers in the crowd, though distant; only the female voices seemed to carry to my listening ears.

"Who is he?"

"I have never heard of him before!"

"He sure speaks well!"

"I wonder if he is married."

I smiled, the happy thought of a woman's company, but the feelings of revenge and my eternal hatred for the men before me pushed those thoughts aside. I remained standing while my guests ate the first and main courses. My mask still hid the smile on my face.

"Now for dessert, sent in from my hometown of Paris," I said, attempting my best French accent, a tongue that I had practiced since I first gave thought to the detailed plan.

As they ate, I felt eyes looking at me, attempting to see beyond the mask. The music stopped when the last forks were laid down.

"Now for some dance. If all would proceed forward to the ballroom floor."

Chairs slid back as men bowed, offering their hands to the women seated beside them. I remained, waiting for all to make their way to the center of the expanse of polished wood. Once all were there, I paced to the front, feeling every head turn to follow my movement.

"If the following could please make their way to the center with their companions for the first dance," I read list of names. The floor cleared as men and women moved aside, allowing for those invited for the first dance. "It is with great honor that I host you all here tonight," I heard the shuffling of feet behind me as my white-clad men entered. They formed two lines, on either side of my special guests.

The music played and the six pairs danced a slow

waltz. At the end of the tune, I held my hand high in the air.

"Ladies and gentlemen, bear witness to the following event, for it will last forever in your minds as a fresh memory; as if it happened only yesterday."

My words seemed to strike their souls — they expected something grand, exquisite; something they've never seen before. And I gave them just that. The white-clad gentlemen reached out to each woman on the dance floor in escort, leaving me with just my betrayers. Several of my sailors moved to their designated locations beside windows, doors, and any other escape routes.

Then it was just this small group, standing before a well-selected crowd. The bars on uniforms, the age of wisdom, and aura of power filled the room. Never before have I been in the presence of such an assembled group of influential beings. Statesmen, lawyers, and politicians; I was just a mere clerk in the grand sense, a messenger of fate.

"My honored guests, have you enjoyed your night thus far?" I allowed them to nod. "Good, I am glad, for it will be your last." I ripped off my mask and threw it down to the floor. I then unsheathed the sword on my hip and smiled.

Bernardo Bermudez stood in shock. I could see the scarlet stone embedded in the ring on his finger from the distance that separated us. My men had their swords pointed at the other guests, prepared to take life if needed, though the plan only called for the deaths of half a dozen.

"Yes, you know my face, you know my name; Hernando Audaz. But things have changed. I escaped the hellish life you had forced upon me. Since then, I have planned for this moment each hour of my existence. Nothing can save you from what is to come!" A series of gasps and shrieks echoed from the side, as my audience was perplexed at the change in events. "Call me Captain Blood Bones, and now do as I say." I placed the tip of my blade to the sternum of my former commanding officer.

"Say it!" I applied enough pressure to draw blood, a red stain appearing through his white linens.

"Ca-captain, B-Blood Bones," he stuttered in fear.

"Good, remember it, for that will be the last name that escapes your worthless lips."

I pushed hard, ending the man's life quickly. I proceeded down the line, slaying each as they begged for dear life. I felt relieved; I bent down, grabbed the limp hand of Bernardo Bermudez and donned his scarlet stone. As I pen this now, I feel my hand write on its own accord, as this very ring has a mind of its own, controlling what I write.

18

June 24, 1763
London, England

As the sun inched above the eastern horizon, Nelson and his officers herded their chosen men and weapons into five carriages. As instructed, all were dressed in the tarred linens of common sailors to avoid drawing attention to their mission. They rode down the length of the quay, the sails and spars of their vessels shrinking with the distance created by every step of the pulling horses. All morning they rode, stopping only once to water and feed the horses and to relieve themselves in trailside bushes. The sun was soon directly overhead, and then descending to the west.

The caravan marched ever onward, in line with Nelson's leading coach. Inside, he sat with his officers as each discussed their hopes and dreams for what would follow once the mission was completed.

"I'd like to lay on my porch swing and sip a nice Scotch-filled glass, enjoying a slow passing and leisurely day. It's been a long while since last I've been home." All eyes were on the captain. Nelson smiled, looking at Ben with a friendly face.

He was in a daze; the melodic ride so relaxing he had to pull himself out of his daydream with both hands. His body still ached from his fall the day before. He blinked several times before realizing that it was his turn to speak. Ben glanced around the carriage, noting that all eyes were on him.

"And what of you, young Benjamin?" Nelson urged him to speak.

"Well," he paused, at a loss for something to say. "Probably find a job shore side; maybe get a place with my brother, Sal, and Jacob. I'm not really sure. I would love to continue sailing and exploring. I'd like to start writing my adventures down. I haven't really thought of much else since the whole Leah and Louisa Ann situation. Everything kind of exploded in my face. I'd like to fix what happened if I can." He stopped speaking; recalling the story his friends had told him of their last run-in with Leah. "She said she never wants to see me again. I just don't understand why she was so upset with me when she basically lead me on, you know?"

"Aye." Charles placed a friendly hand on Ben's knee. "You may very well never understand what a woman thinks or why she says the things she says. I feel the seas and oceans are more predictable than even the most foreseeable woman, and even then, you are battling the worst and heaviest seas God can throw at you."

Nate smiled. "Try not to think too much into things, just focus on what is, not what if or what was."

"Well spoken, on all accounts," Nelson said. He paused for a minute, allowing the silence to end the previous discussion. "You are in company of men fit for duty, and full of courage not seen in any ordinary man. We shall succeed; I know it. But for now, we are just a few minutes away from a tavern. We will feed our hunger and drink ourselves well. We will dine like the kings we are and know we are. To this, I toast," he held up an imaginary glass.

Each hand cupped nothing but air, and as the laughter ensued, the carriages made their way along the wooded edges of Sherwood Forest. The noise of chirping birds singing their songs, joined with the steady fall of horse hooves, created a symphony of natural wonder and beauty, as the caravan traveled along the well-worn path.

✖✖✖✖

The five drivers reined the teams of horses to a stop. Men emerged from each coach and congregated in a circle on the cobblestoned lane in the small town. They walked around stretching out the kinks in their bodies. All were exhausted from the long ride. After the mares of their team were tied to a watering post, Nelson and his officers led the remaining men to the inn's entrance.

A cloud of smoke wafted out, as the door was held open for all to pass through. Nelson led the way, asking the owner for rooms for the night.

"Aye, sir, I'll have them made up nice and neat for you all. There's a few tables available over there also." He pointed.

"Thank you, kind sir." Nelson smiled, nodding to the man.

They wove their way around other crowded tables, full of drunken wanderers and outcasts. Laughter and singing filled the room as the group took several outlaying stools and took their seats at a few grand tables in the corner of the tavern. A serving maid came out with a pitcher of ale and a stack of mugs. Her eyes passed from man to man as she remembered their food orders.

The group ate and drank heartily, content with full stomachs and slurred speech. One by one, the men trickled up to the rooms upstairs to fall into a deep, relaxing sleep before the upcoming day. Ben remained, quietly staring at his half empty glass, carefully laying out the railroad ties as his Memory Express pulled to the platform of Reality.

Harris caught his attention with a quick jab of a fork. "Wake up, sunshine."

"Huh?" He was unaware he had been staring off into space for the last hour.

"Dude, I was waving, clapping, and yelling but you were completely out of it."

"Oh," Ben replied. "I guess I'm just thinking about tomorrow, you know, hoping everything goes as planned." He was also thinking of losing Leah, this time forever. The thoughts of possibly losing Louisa Ann before he technically had her also caused him grief. He stretched out the aches and pains that spread through his body.

"Yeah, I thought about that for a little, but then I discovered delicious food and thirst quenching drink." Harris laughed.

Ben smiled, aware that Sal and Jacob had also remained at the table to keep him company. The other men had all gone to their rooms for some shut-eye.

"It's just this whole mission feels weird, you know? I thought privateers captured pirates ships and plundered enemy fortresses," Ben paused to collect his thoughts. "You know, that sort of thing."

"And they do, we do. So what's your point?" Sal laughed.

"I don't know; it's just that I don't have a good feeling about running through the woods of Sherwood Forest trying to assassinate one of the country's leaders."

Harris looked at his brother with a mocking eye. "Come on, did we know Mad Dog, Blood Spot, or Blood Bones?"

Ben sighed. He knew that they were right and that there was no point to argue.

Harris continued. "I know what it is! You are just afraid of Robin Hood and his band of merry men!"

"Ha, very funny," Ben said through gritted teeth.

Sal edged closer to the table. He looked at the brothers and their similar features, and then to Jacob. Finally he said, "Guys, we are Robin Hood and the merry men! We'll lay this trap upon Grenville, clean our hands of everything and then retire as rich, young men," he paused. "Just think of all those treasure chests from our last adventure. We got enough between the four of us to build a castle of gold."

Ben looked at Sal, shaking his head. "Yeah, I guess. You know that I'd be Robin, right?"

Sal leaned across rows of empty dishes and mugs, puckering up for a kiss.

"And I'd be Maid Marian." He reached out to grab Ben's collar.

Their laughter echoed throughout the busy tavern. One by one, Nelson's men retired for a sleepless night. All were anxious and excited for the next chapter of their adventure.

✖✖✖

*L*eah awoke to an empty bed, to an empty room and to an empty world.

Her husband must have left for business some time long before the sun had risen. The new day's light filtered into the luxurious hotel room between open drapes. She stretched, yawning after a long night of tossing and turning.

Leah looked round the room, realizing the closet was now missing all of her husband's weapons and his uniform. She thought this odd for the early hour, and slowly moved from under the warmth of the woolen covers.

Pacing to the nearby table, she saw a carelessly scribbled note there. Reading quickly, she then discarded the message with a sigh. If she was to ever get over Ben, and on with her new life, her husband should have been present, but even with that small and remote request, she'd been left alone, staring out the window at the dead street below.

She could count the traffic of persons transiting the cobbled street on a single hand. Something was odd, she thought. An unusual foreboding overwhelmed her, and she broke down in a hysterical fit of tears. All that she had ever hoped and dreamt for seemed so far away now; she felt lost in a world of regret as the only thing she knew was memories of young love on the verge of collapse.

19

June 25, 1763
Sherwood Forest

Prime Minister George Grenville took a deep breath as he sighted Sherwood Forest a quarter mile down the windy path at the crest of a hill. He looked out the carriage window and saw the unchanging scene below. Every year at this time he and his extended family would meet for a weeklong hunting excursion in the woods. Clouds filled a majority of the sky, casting a dark gloom upon the green shrubbery lining the well-walked path through Sherwood. A lone horseman guided the way for the single carriage, which today carried only Grenville and a close family friend. As the travelers made their way to the wooded edge, a flock of flapping birds flew out from the treetops, leaving the woods barren of life and chirping song.

※※※

Ben pressed the telescope to his eyes as he leaned with his chest flush against the tree. Slowly his gaze scanned the horizon of windswept grass and dirt paths. The rolling hills hid some of the animal trails that led to the entrance to Sherwood, but after several moments, the head of a lone horseman escorting a single carriage came into view.

"I've just sighted Grenville; it looks to be about a quarter-mile or less until his carriage passes below us," he called down to five men below.

On cue, Jacob ran off to meet with Marconi at the southern fork of the trail. They had surveyed and mapped the forest, learning of the single entrance, but also of the many smaller paths that lay within the wood. Of these, Nathan and his group of Irajan warriors searched each path, memorizing the trends and impressions upon which horse and men had traveled. The plan was simple: block the southern course and force Grenville to take the northern path. This northern route had the widest berth of all, which would seem the best path for Grenville to follow, and also the most direct trail to the wooden bridge that spanned Sherwood's fast flowing river. Nelson's men had wandered all morning through the nooks and crannies of the area, discovering hollow trees in which to hide, and small cave-like depressions in the earth from which to take aim. Messages had been relayed and the southern route had been blocked and covered with shrubberies. Their combined and focused efforts made the trail appear to vanish all together.

✖✖✖

As the lone horseman made his way through the thicket, his curious eyes strained in the darkness of Sherwood to discover the well-worn path they would take to cross the river. The man remained a dozen paces ahead of the carriage, but as his horse shied at eerie forest noises, naturally slowing down, the carriage closed the distance between them.

"Come on! If we're to make it to the other end of the woods by nightfall we'll need to make haste," the carriage driver called to the escort.

He turned his head, yelling over his shoulder. "The horse is hesitant, we shall proceed with caution. She's been through these woods more than I have!"

Their travel was slow, both horse and man unwilling to venture forward without trepidation.

✖.✖.✖

*A*fter the carriage and lead horseman had moved deeper into the woods, diverting to the northern route as hoped, Ben and his remaining four men slowly crept in the shadows until they passed the barricade of the southern path. There, they remained on a straight course, taking a deer trail to one of the oldest trees in all of Sherwood. This tree overlooked the river below, and from its heights Ben could see Nelson's troops on the far shore, Brodkin's men on the northern border, and Marconi and his troop to the south.

As the cloud-hidden sun slowly made its way to the western sky, the carriage and lone horseman exited through a patch of the wooded edge. There they waited, looking out into the river and its bubbling foam. Along with the swaying limbs of treetops on a steady wind, the sound of a nearby waterfall created a natural symphony for all of the forest to hear.

George Grenville exited the carriage, soon followed by his close friend. The two scanned the bridge, the surrounding water, and the foliage on the opposing bank.

"Ah, yet another year passed," he said to his friend.

The man turned to the prime minister. "Aye. It's another mark upon the calendar that is life. We've another hour of riding before we meet up with the rest of your family. Let us water the horses first."

They passed their request to the leadsman and the carriage driver. After allowing the beasts a long drink from the cool water, the group continued the trip and made their way along the rocks to the base of the wooden bridge. The echo of horseshoes upon the wood sounded across the stretch of open area. From their hiding place, all of Nelson's men were eager to commence the next phase of what would be their last mission serving under King George III.

As the horseman and carriage were at the halfway point across the bridge, Nathan and five Irajan warriors crept out cautiously from the shadows. They stood low, hunched along the low wooden hand-rails. The distance between the carriage and them grew as it moved toward the eastern shore. Nelson fired a warning shot from deep within the wooded edge. The horses pulled backward, unsure of the shot's origin.

For his part, Brodkin led his troops south through the churn-ing river water, careful to not step in any holes or slip on any rocks. Meanwhile, heading north, Marconi was doing the same. Ben sat perched upon the giant tree's limb, projecting their movements and the plan's outcome. His hands moved about him, orchestrating the men below with a smile as all fronts soon closed upon one point.

❉❉❉

After hearing the gunshot George Grenville slid the window open slightly, allowing for a quick gaze to the northern side of the bridge. There his eyes took in the quick flowing water splashing against the rocks, and a group of five common-clothed men making their way toward him. He edged the window open further and looked forward, seeing more men with their guns raised. He felt the wheels beneath him cease their spinning as the carriage came to a halt.

"You might as well surrender; you are surrounded on all sides!" Nelson screamed to the entrapped men over the sounds of the flow-ing water.

With guns and arrows pointed at him from all angles, the car-riage driver remained motionless. The lead horseman had retraced his steps, moving closer to the carriage for what little protection it would afford him.

He called out to the men who surrounded him. "This carriage belongs to the Prime Minister. Let us pass or there will be hell to pay!" The wary man pulled out a small handgun from inside his coat. He cocked it and held it high above his head, ready to take aim.

❉❉❉

A wave of British Royal Army soldiers rushed into the edge of Sherwood Forest from the hilly countryside. Rows and rows of men filtered in, making their way down the path. Their scouts traced each route and soon lay well out of sight from their naval counterparts. Captain Richard Highmore looked out, seeing the bridge to the north, and men on the opposing bank. He had only minutes if he were to entrap Nelson and his men: dog cornering the cat, cornering the mouse. Of course, he had other motives than to just surround these men, he wished to slay as many as possible, leaving perhaps only Ben alive to witness his brutality. The thought of insufferable pain and bloodshed put a large smile on his face. His red locks slithered atop his head as he made his way quickly, leading his men through the many paths of Sherwood.

✖✖✖

There was another warning shot.

Nelson was serious, unwilling to give up his position to the group of four men. He scanned the carriage, looking for the prime minister, but the man would not leave the safety of the interior.

"Let us make this as painless as possible," the leader of the brigands called out for all to hear.

The lead horseman took aim and with a pull of the trigger, felled a man who stood beside Nelson. As the horseman readied for another shot, Nelson's men, surrounding him, moved closer, stepping forward several feet. Their trap had been set; there was no possible route for escape atop the bridge. The prime minister was as sure as dead.

But then in the corner of his eye, Ben saw the glimmer of sun on metal. A break in the clouds above yielded this forewarning, and as he strained his eyes, he saw a flank of redcoats making their way down the opposing bank, heading toward the backs of Nelson's men. He shifted his weight, leaning to the right to gaze at the southern approach. More redcoats came into view as they moved to encircle

Marconi and his men. Somehow knowledge of this mission had leaked out. It would not be so easy now; they were outnumbered at least two to one.

As Ben was about to climb down, he heard a gunshot from below. A man fell holding his chest as a wave of redcoats filtered in, surrounding the tree. His men below fought back, sending off shots as they took cover in nearby foliage. Ben hugged the tree, hoping he was not sighted. He was not discovered, and though he had momentarily escaped death, he was still trapped. He looked down, watching ten redcoats check the dead and injured. They moved quickly, heading eastward toward the bridge and the water's edge.

After feeling it was safe to come down from the tree, Ben ran along a game trail in pursuit. He did not care if he would be heard; he had to warn his friends and fellow sailors of the turn of events. Every second counted, every second meant the possible survival of his shipmates. He turned a sharp corner around a large boulder nearly running into the tail end of the squad of redcoats who had just slain his party of men.

With a jerk of his rifle, he sent the butt across the back of the nearest soldier's head. The man howled in pain as he fell to his knees. A soldier in front heard the scrapple, causing Ben to let loose another powerful blow, knocking the man flat to his stomach. Turning quickly, he pursued the remaining men. One at a time, he managed to stop their progress between bouts of one-on-one combat. He emerged from the woods, staring at the bridge and the surrounding waters.

Ben's hard training had paid off.

Gunfire erupted from all corners, and men fell, holding their open wounds. On all fronts, redcoats pressed Nelson and his men into the churning river waters. Two hunting rifles emerged from the slits in the carriage windows, shooting into the rows of exposed backs.

He quickly took sight of the area; Jacob to his right fighting alongside Marconi, Sal on the opposing shore beside Nelson, and his brother to his left next to Brodkin. For the moment, his closest friends were safe. He released a quick sigh of relief as he trudged forward. He took aim with his rifle, felling a man from fifty yards.

Clouds of black smoke rose from each barrel as men fired and reloaded. It was a slaughter. There was no retreat and nowhere to go besides fight in the churning waters. The redcoats continued their pressure, forcing all to the confines of the wooden bridge.

Ben looked around once more, taking sight of a man with a raised barrel. He looked across the battlefield, seeing his target. A cringe of pain rang through his heart, as the man readied a shot at Jacob, for fear of his friend's life. He moved forward instinctively, without thinking, running through the thigh-deep water, hoping to slay the man before Jacob could be shot. His progress was slow as he waded through the deepest part of the river. The water was nearly chest high now. Taking swift aim, he let off a shot. His round whizzed through the air but missed his target, but it was enough to delay the man's own shot at Jacob.

As the waters became shallow toward the shore, Ben came to the rescue as he swung the rifle around his head. He brought wooden stock down against the hands of Jacob's attacker just as he had finished priming the pan on his own weapon. Jacob managed to side-step quickly and plunge his sword into his enemy's stomach.

There was no time for words, but Jacob nodded his thanks and between the two, they covered the southern approach, allowing for several of Marconi's men to step onto dry land. A fight within the confines of the river would mean certain death; to stand upon solid ground would at least give them a fighting chance.

Ten minutes into the battle, Nelson ordered his men into a formation that pushed forward to the east. They moved in this formation, keeping their backs to one another and their rifles pointed toward their enemies. Nearly all were on solid ground when a loud eruption ripped through the group of men.

✖✖✖✖

*B*en smiled as he saw his brother still alive. He was amidst his own one-on-one battle. As Ben continued his trek forward, he took a tally of how many of his men had been slain. His shock dissipated when a grenade had been hurled down from a tree and the explosion tore through breeches and skin, felling several men nearby.

Harris was still making his way to the eastern shore along with several stragglers when he felt a tear in his shoulder. Blood spurted out from the bullet wound as the lead shrapnel separated skin from bone. He dropped forward, falling face first into the water. The current took hold of him as his body was dragged downstream. From the corner of his eye, he watched the ensuing battle pass by as he continued his helpless escape in the churning waters.

Of the thirty-two men Nelson commanded when the skirmish began, his quick count now found only ten. All his officers were still alive and fighting bravely. He called to his men and then led the way through the thick foliage, jumping over the low bushes lining the river. As the group entered the woods, another front of redcoats blocked their escape. A perfectly timed volley passed through them and two more men dropped to the ground, screaming in agony. Nelson turned right, following the river to the south, but again there were no openings to their advantage in the enemy rank.

The eight men remaining men were quickly surrounded and disarmed. They were herded together like common animals. Pushed with the butts of the redcoats' rifles, they were tied together with a long length of line. After they were forced to cross the wooden bridge to the west, they emerged before the rolling hillside of green windswept grass. A dozen carriages and horses stood awaiting the redcoats and their prisoners. The evening sky was filled with a color similar to that which had stained the grounds of Sherwood Forest and the churning waters that coiled through the woods.

✖✖✖

The fast flowing waters carried his body downstream through a slalom course of rocks. Harris slowly became aware of the sound of an approaching waterfall. The sound carried up the thirty-foot descent from below, and as he looked up from his roughly moving place in the water, he realized his body was just at the edge. He somersaulted between jutting rocks, making a large splash in the pooled waters below. After resurfacing and bouts of heavy breathing, he regained his composure and struggled to swim to the edge of the river against the strong current. He pulled his body to the side, longing to live. Finally, he crawled out, his body completely exhausted from the ordeal he had just been through. After a while, his breath steadied, and he stood up slowly.

Harris trudged through the thick vegetation, keeping to the eastward shore. After fifteen minutes of arduous trekking, he saw the backs of a row of redcoats pushing several prisoners along on the opposing shore. He waited until no other redcoats were in sight and then pushed forward to the water's edge. Harris looked around; hoping someone would have been overlooked and alive, but from what he could see, all of Nelson's fallen men had been killed or taken prisoner. He stood there for a moment, taking in the sight of the ill-fated battle. With one last sigh, he rushed to where they had kept their mares and wagons. Slashing the ropes that restrained each horse, he set the animals free except for one white horse. The mare seemed eager for what Harris knew would be a long night.

A lone figure rode out of Sherwood Forest, keeping just out of sight behind the line of red coats.

✖✖✖

All were quiet within the tight quarters of the wagon. Nelson and his men had been thrown inside, and since departing Sherwood, each man kept his thoughts to himself. Ben moved to the side, staring at the rolling hills that passed by through the barred window. At times, when the caravan was in the trough of a hill, he thought he saw a glimmer of a figure atop a white mare off in the distance, maintaining a steady distance behind.

✵✵✵

Leah had spent the entire day walking the streets of London alone. At times, she would shiver from a cold sea breeze that followed the River Thames and spread through the windy cobblestoned lanes of the city. Her heart had been in a maze, running confused and bumping into the high, constricting emotional hedge that is adolescence. She ate an evening meal at an outdoor café, reading a pamphlet of the plays and of a circus that would be coming shortly to town. She sighed, knowing she would likely attend these events by herself. Her husband was off on some errand, and she was once again unsure of when he would return. Her vacation seemed nearly permanent; she was beginning to forget her residence in South Downs and accepted the London scenery.

She passed under a setting sun; the light shimmered along the worn stones that her feet gently grazed. She made her way back to the room she had been staying in the past several days and once inside, sat beside the window. Twilight battled the heavens and slowly stars speckled the darkened sky. She sat there, her blond hair falling beside the curves of her gentle and smooth cheeks. Transfixed, she stared off into space, noting the occasional drunkard as he exited a tavern or a tar-clothed sailor heading toward the wharf.

The opening of the room's door interrupted her dreams of Ben and the happiness he'd instilled in her. Visions of the handsome young man seemed to linger on the features of the man who stood before her, but his fiery red hair was not the same as Ben's dark mane.

"My dearest Leah, let us retire for the night. I have a pleasant surprise for you tomorrow," Captain Richard Highmore said with a twisted smile. "Of which, I will most certainly enjoy your presence at."

20

June 26, 1763
London, England

Quick on the heels of the prime minister, Captain Richard Highmore wore a large and sinister smile. Rapping a knuckle upon the heavy door before him, Grenville awaited the invitation to enter from the High Council. The door slowly creaked open to allow the two figures passage into the amphitheater. Highmore looked around, imagining a full crowd of witnesses as Benjamin Manry and his unfortunate accomplices pleaded their case before the jury, though of course, he mused, Ben had been caught in the act of treason and would be sentenced to death by hanging. His smile grew ever larger as he realized he was so close to his goal of removing Ben from Leah's life forever.

"Ah! Prime Minister George Grenville, it is so very good to see you. It has been quite a while, has it not?" the first councilman said.

"Yes, it has been since the last trial, many months ago. I am here on a more serious matter, but for similar reasons."

"Go on." The man nodded, his white and powdered wig shifting slightly on his head. He gestured with an arm and led the way into the chamber. "Let us take our seats."

A group of twelve men, all in their later years of life, sat discussing the events that had taken place less than a day earlier.

"So, you wish for a hearing at first light?" The head council spoke in a raspy voice.

Grenville shook his head. "A hearing at first light? Nonsense. There is no need for I would like to sleep in after the ordeal I had been through. However, I do wish for a hanging at noon. Their deaths will be at the gallows. They are guilty, each and every one of them. If it were not for the assistance of this brave individual and his men, I surely would've met my maker face to face."

All eyes turned to Highmore. His crooked smile sent shivers down the councilmen's spines, whether or not he might be deemed a hero.

"And what a fine service you did for England, Captain Highmore! By the way, how did you fall upon this rescue?"

Highmore closed his eyes, memories of the past week filtered into his mind, and he simply replied with a mischievous grin. "Oh, just plain old luck, I suppose."

With that, the fate of the eight captured men was decided as if one had flipped a one-sided coin.

✹✹✹

The grounds of Buckingham Palace remained quiet as King George III sat at his telescope, his gaze upon the celestial bodies above. The craters upon the moon's surface smiled back at him, the belt of Orion sparkled brightly, and the pointer stars of the Big Dipper led the way to Polaris. He let out a deep sigh at the wondrous view, completely overtaken by the night sky's beauty. The sound of a fast-moving horse and buggy below captured his attention. He watched the man exit the buggy and rush quickly toward the gate guardsmen. After a brief discussion and several hand motions to signal his urgency, the messenger was allowed passage into the palace. The king remained at his window, knowing that this message would either bring news of the success or failure of the daring mission.

✹✹✹

Louisa Ann sat atop her horse for a midnight ride. A slight blanket of clouds cradled the moon and she sighed at the beauty that surrounded her. It had been several days since she had last seen Ben and all her thoughts were of him. She often pictured them together, holding hands and walking along the River Thames on beautiful sun-filled days. A large smile formed on her face as she rode slowly across the grounds.

In the distance, she saw the front gate open for a messenger. She thought it odd that at such a late hour one would call upon her cousin. After she led her horse back to the stable and released it to the care of a sleepy groom, she quickly made her way to the back entrance of Buckingham Palace.

✖✖✖

"Yes, yes come in," the king replied to the messenger.

A young man opened the door, slipped through and quickly made his way to the far window. The door behind him remained open several inches.

"My king, I am stationed at the dungeons of the White Tower. I bear news of the mission; a group of eight were led and shackled below." He stopped to catch his breath. "There was a heated discussion amongst the High Officials and it seems that our men will be tried for conspiracy in the assassination attempt of Prime Minister George Grenville. They will be hung in the courtyard at noon!"

King George III remained staring through his telescope, disbelieving the recent turn in events.

"How is this possible?"

"My king, we are not sure. I overheard a man mention the name Captain Richard Highmore. I believe him to be an officer of the Royal Army."

The king looked away from the celestial waltz that spanned the heavens and adjusted his position in his seat. "How many survivors were there?"

The messenger frowned. "Just the men that were brought in, eight so far that we know of, your majesty. Rumor is there was a slaughter in Sherwood Forest. Nelson and his three officers are among those alive, but there have been no names released for fear of their association with you, my king."

George remained quiet, thinking of how such a carefully laid out plan could have failed. After a long period of silence, he concluded that the evening's troubles were not due to the fault of his men, but due to the actions of Richard Highmore.

The name rung a bell. At the numerous parties and galas he had attended over the years, a fiery-headed army man had been present and now came to the king's mind. There had been a conversation shared with the man and a brief introduction to his young wife. He remembered the woman's gaze at Benjamin, and how he'd seen them as they talked in whispers. It began to make sense — he then wondered if it were possible that this man had somehow learned of the mission.

His fist pounded the table beside him. The telescope shook with the vibration brought about by his anger.

"Bloody Hell!" he cursed aloud.

Louisa Ann stood at the entranceway. She had just overheard of the capture of her newfound love, and of the trial and certain hanging at first light. She broke down in tears, and ran from the observation room to her bedchamber.

He dismissed the messenger and resumed his stargazing. As the moon came into sight once more, he strained his eyes and the craters appeared to change to a deep red color. Upon the moon's surface, he imagined the afternoon's battlefield covered in blood. There was nothing he could do to protect Nelson and his men, nothing to save then, nothing to delay their hearing. He was in a bind, to defend his men from what happened would link the assassination plot to him, and it would destroy him politically. Even as king of a country, his power was limited in this circumstance.

"I suppose all is fair in love and war," he whispered to the stars above, thinking of the failed conspiracy and of young Louisa Ann's affection for Ben.

❈❈❈

*B*en paced the dungeon cell anxiously. The smell of human decay overwhelmed him. The trial and death at the gallows haunted his mind. A voice hailed him from across the cell.

"Come, take a seat, there is nothing you or I can do now."

He looked at Nelson and smiled weakly. "I suppose. What of King George III? Will he be able to save us?"

Nelson shrugged. "Most likely our names will not be mentioned nor knowledge of our dealings with the king. He cannot admit to the assassination attempt. The king would not risk it. No barrister would take our case, and in fact, they might even skip the hearing. What evidence do we have to defend ourselves?"

Ben nodded gloomily. "I suppose you are right." He began to think of the figure he had seen following the caravan on its way back to London. "Captain, I believe Harris still lives."

Nelson shifted his position against the stone behind him. "Are you sure? I saw him shot. I believe he fell into the water and was carried away."

Ben closed his eyes, picturing the scene Nelson described. "Yes, but I saw a figure atop a white horse following us the entire way back. When we were in a valley he was atop the hill and then he would disappear. I'm sure of it. It was Harris."

"How sure are you?" Nelson suddenly became serious and optimistic at the possibility of a rescue.

"Positive. I know my brother; I would have done the same if I were in his shoes. What if he was injured but only to a small extent? Why continue the battle if he saw a chance for escape and for the chance of our rescue? You've taught us well. He is smart— I believe he still is alive."

"Perhaps then there is still chance for an escape! Keep close to the window, maybe you will hear something."

Their chances were slim for eavesdropping, as only small vents and tunnels led to the main street above. Even moonlight struggled to filter in through these channels, but wafts of fresh air occasionally made their way into the putrid-smelling dungeon. The eight men resumed their sluggish wandering through the small cell. Their chains restricted quick movement and all were tired from the day's events, but Nelson remained sitting and thinking. There was a bulge inside his chest pocket, and he remembered that he had the crimson journal tucked inside. Though dim, the glow from a single candle overhead produced enough light to read the scrawling penmanship of Captain Blood Bones.

January 5, 1752

We refitted our ship; bringing on heavier guns for the battle to come, hiring hundreds of men, and obtaining new provisions. How was I to steal Drake's treasure from the depths of El Morro? I hope I shall soon figure out — I will meet with Sesostris soon, anticipating a new wave of images to come in the prophecy. I have much to be proud of in these last months.

Sesostris entered my quarters with the crystal ball held snug in his arms. As has become our custom, he removed the cloth wrapping and placed it on the table before me.

"Are you ready?" he asked.

I nodded, placing my hands on the base, and channeled my thoughts into the orb. My body shook a moment as I envisioned a series of stairwells leading down, spiraled into the depths below a dungeon level. Hundreds of feet down it went, until at last I emerged into a cavern full to the brink of capacity. The image sifted through aisles and stacks of chests, rugs, and bags of coins. Sir Francis Drake's treasure was now mine. In one lone chest lay a staff. Again, like the map I had viewed earlier, I stared down at my writing on the notes that had lain hidden inside the staff. Three medallions sat beside, and my vision suddenly changed.

Looking at the coast of the New World as if from high in the sky, I fell slowly to the earth. I saw the islands of the Caribbean, the familiar jutting shape of Florida, and then the city of St. Augustine. There was a river leading inland from the sea, zigzagging through the terrain, and the waterway opened onto a large egg-shaped island. Two large rocks marked the landing and I followed a path, seeing three young adventurers entering the bowels of a crooked-faced cave.

I now knew of the location, I just had to find it after my sack of El Morro. As my vision faded away, my immortality curse was now within reach: the staff to hold the curse, the medallions to carry my three saviors, my crimson journal to hide the secret, and the scarlet stone upon my finger. These are the four items that I now know I must possess, but as I look down, I come to the end of the last page in my journal.

🟐🟐🟐

Sunrise broke the spell of the night, and the last shadow of darkness left the cobblestoned streets of London. Commoners walked about as usual; a group of passerby moved slowly past the empty platform at the town's center, carrying their day's wares. On a post a notice was tacked, announcing the execution of the traitors at noon. With every inch the sun angled upward in the sky, families and strangers alike came together.

🟐🟐🟐

The sound of ringing church bells signaled noon. A line of drummers marched into the courtyard. They played a steady beat as men boxed the gallows. Once all were in position, the drums ceased playing, allowing for a silence to spread through the crowd. A loud bugle sounded the arrival of the royal family and select members of high importance.

In the crook of his arm, Leah walked alongside her husband. Her beauty contrasted to his repulsiveness, truly an example of beauty and the beast. She held her head high, keeping a fake smile upon her lips, a smile she was growing used to. It had been a while since she flashed a genuine smile, at least since her last evening with Ben and his friends. Knowing something more than she understood was amiss, she began to cringe with fear at the surprise her husband had promised.

The crowd bowed as their leader made his way to the designated seats overlooking the gallows. Leah's place was mere feet from that of Louisa Ann, each thinking the other unaware of their shared affection for Benjamin Manry. One already knew of the failed mission and winced in pain at being present at the hangings; the other was expecting a surprise she feared would not be pleasant.

The drums began their slow and steady beat as the group of prisoners was prodded forward with the tips of swords, their ankle chains causing them to shuffle with each step. All eight wore filthy robes. Bloodstains and dirt crusted to their faces. Most were hardly recognizable, at least from afar. To discover their true identities one would have to gaze closely.

All stood before their respective noose. The drums ceased again as the bugle played, its tune quieting the crowd. A line of black-robed men approached the platform. A priest and his altar boy stood off to the side, waiting their turn for speech. The prime minister twitched with anticipation for the event to begin, and Highmore beamed an evil smile, knowing that he would soon witness the love of Leah's life dangling at the end of a rope.

She glanced down from their lofty perch, scanning the crowd. A young man moved quickly through the masses, pushing and shoving people out of his way. After catching several glimpses of the man, Leah recognized the familiar face of Harris approaching with haste. Her stomach cringed and then she looked at the faces of each man standing atop the platform below.

Her husband nudged her elbow, "It seems you are looking for something? Well, if you look carefully at the fourth man from the left, you will soon become aware of why I brought you here. You see, I simply could not trust you; you're young, beautiful, and foolish. Well, mainly foolish, I daresay. Not to question your youth and beauty. I had a man follow you, and I was well aware of your meetings with your secret lover. I learned of their plans, and then soon developed my own, a scheme to tear apart your heart so I can have it all to myself. To rebuild a palace by demolishing its foundations and starting over," his words soon faded as her eyes focused upon Ben's features for what she thought would be the last time.

"You animal! You are despicable!"

She stood up briskly, hearing the laughter of Captain Richard Highmore carry over the crowd's cheers as she ran away from her husband. All of the negative thoughts for Ben over the past few days had vanished instantly the second she thought she might lose him forever. Tears began to form at the corners of her eyes.

❋❋❋

All night Harris had traveled atop the white horse, following a line of carriages through the English countryside to the city of London. He ached from the pain in his shoulder and his eyes drooped from the lack of sleep. His body swayed back and forth as the horse slowly stopped, overlooking the bank of the mighty River Thames. He swung off the saddle, moving as quickly as his legs could carry him. The sounds of bells, drums, and bugles grew louder as he emerged into a large courtyard. In the distance he could see a platform with eight men standing, facing the mob of Londoners.

Two figures moved through the crowd, heading for the same edge of the gallows. They fought through the packed courtyard; every second would count if either were to say their last good-byes. Harris caught sight of his brother through a break in the mass of bodies, but soon crashed into someone on the move, almost knocking her off her feet.

Leah stood tall, brushing her dress back as she sniffed away tears. "Harris, tell me what happened!"

He looked at her, unsure of how to break the news, or even where to start. Before speaking he looked around, standing perhaps a dozen feet away from Ben and his shipmates.

"A well thought-out plan took a turn for the worse. Somehow information of it leaked out," Harris said.

Leah grabbed hold of his palm, bringing both of her gloved hands around his. "My husband was behind it all. He had a spy follow me. He has meant to torture me, to break my heart into a million pieces," she paused, another wave of crying washed over her. "Is there anything left that we can do?"

Harris stared out at the many guards surrounding the perimeter of the courtyard.

"To fight would certainly mean death for you and I, as well as everyone already on the gallows."

He shook his head.

"Attention all citizens of London, all dwellers of England, today the twenty-sixth day of June in the year of our lord, 1763, we are here to bear witness the testimonies of the men who stand before us all. They were caught in the midst of an assassination attempt upon the Prime Minister George Grenville, in the shadows of Sherwood Forest." The black robed man let his booming voice carry. His veil hung low over his face. He continued. "These men are filthy outcasts from society. If ever there was a time in their lives that they had been respected it was quite a while ago. They are guilty. To attempt such an act against a leader of our great country is like attempting to take the life of the king himself! God protect the King!" He paused, hearing the echoed chant through the crowd. "I say these men are guilty, and shall be cursed to their deaths by hanging."

Several whoops of joy and the prospect of entertainment rang through the crowd. As the man began reading the death sentence, a group of translators and reporters began writing down the speech and sketching drawings of the event for headlines in the following morning's paper. Translators spoke out loudly in French, Italian, and Spanish; the words creating a diverse verbal symphony upon the platform as the crowd cheered for the execution to start.

"...*como* Las *multitudes chillaron fuera, algunos oran que* El *perdón para los ocho hombres acerca de cuelgue para la traición. otros gritan fuera para sus muertes, una muerte lenta e inevitable. seguro, los* pAgadores *de impuesto son trastornados con las indulgencias recientes de primer ministro, pero quizás estos* Hombres *trataron de tomar cosas en propias las manos. cualquier su historia es, ellos no* IO *estarán compartiendo en comida nocturna,* paRa *las baterías empieza su golpe const*Ante *mas otra vez. sus autorizaciones y las oraciones son leídas, pero entonces hay un viento rápido que lleva a través de la* plataforMa. *las batas son erizadas como un rasgones deslumbradores de* lA *luz por la mu*Ltitud. *yo, yo mismo, me caí hacia atrás como tropecé en el temor. o trabajo de la magia o el* Diablo *que yo no puedo dec*Ir, *pero en ese destello de energía dos* Cuerpos *desaparecieron. seis quedado, columpiando sin vida como la multitud chilló* EN *la incredulidad en el espectáculo,* lA *naranja y desvanecer amarillo de resplandor lentamente en este día, 26 Junio,* 1763."

With that said, a glow of orange and yellow light escaped from the medallions, as well as the crimson journal hidden in Nelson's pocket. Their interwoven fates yet again entwined as the lights linked together, forming a cone of energy in the warping of space and time, setting forth the second phase of the curse of Captain Blood Bones.

21

Modern Day
Boston Museum, Massachusetts

Two guards sat behind the main security desk, sipping their morning coffee and reading their newspapers. One looked up at the clock above his head. He sighed. "Well, damn Bob, it's only seven. We still have another hour to go before we get relieved."

"Yeah, Sam, I know; it's the same routine every time. Do you want to do the last round?"

Sam shook his head and Bob shrugged, sipping at his cup for one last caffeine rush before exploring the nooks and crannies of the quiet museum. "Fine, I'll take it. My legs are falling asleep anyways."

"Way to make excuses. You could also use the exercise!" Sam mocked his friend.

"Very funny." Bob smiled. "Actually the wife got me walking a few times a week with her and Scruffy."

"I suppose the round will only add to your abundant exercise routine."

The guard shook his head, a smile forming on his lips. "If only we hadn't been working this shift together for so long, I would've made you part of the museum by now!"

"Oh, what exhibit?" Sam laughed.

"Probably the Sphinx and Pharaohs, you'd look good under wraps, you know. Then no one would see your ugly face." He stood up and gave a friendly tap on his buddy's shoulder as he made his way down the hall.

Bob's flashlight pierced the darkness of each exhibit. All exterior doors were locked from within and all windows were closed with the shades down. He heard the air conditioning vibrate overhead; the steady hum of fans soothed his mood. His gaze moved around casually; after all, how could anything or anyone get inside without setting off an alarm?

✖✖✖

A violent whirlwind of energy dashed quickly through the museum's eastern wing. A blinding orange and yellow light escaped a three-foot staff that sat quietly inside an exhibit. Four bodies crashed to the ground, their robes and gown fluttering in the supernatural wind. With one last boom of sound and energy, the wind receded and the blinding lights faded.

They lay in a circle, their faces in shock as they expected to hear the click of a gear and utter their last guttural scream before a noose choked the life out of them. Sal and Captain Nelson reached for their necks, feeling for a rope that had just been there, but now wasn't. The glow of three medallions slowly dwindled in intensity, but the warmth on their chests felt odd, yet soothing. Nelson, for his part, reached into his breast pocket, pulling out a glowing crimson journal.

"Where are we?" Sal asked, looking from puzzled face to puzzled face.

Nelson blinked multiple times, unable to comprehend the change of scene. Leah sat still, her breathing out of control in a fit of panic.

Harris stood slowly, looking around the nearest exhibit. He took a couple steps forward, wobbling from the pain that seared throughout his body. He read the sign that hung over the glass display.

"Pirates and Privateers," he mumbled for all could hear.

Harris stared inside the display, looking at a collection of weapons and coins from the eighteenth century. Common tools and coils of line sat inside. His gaze then shifted to a glowing magical staff. He knew this piece well; it was the same staff he and his friends had discovered so many months ago. It now seemed a lifetime ago. A wave of emotion flooded his eyes. Yet again, the medallion around his neck had brought him through the line of time; though he was not sure exactly where he was, or even more important than that, *when.*

He heard a cough and a sniffle from behind, but he continued looking into the display case, staring at an article headlined, June 26, 1763, Conspiracy in the King's Court.

"Oh my God, you won't believe this." Harris pressed his face to the glass display.

"What is it, Harris?" Nelson placed a hand on his shoulder.

"It's an article about what just happened. About our capture and execution. I'll read it to you guys." Harris cleared his throat. "As the crowds screamed out, some prayed for forgiveness for the eight men about to hang for treason. Others yelled for their deaths. Although the taxpayers were upset with Prime Minister George Grenville's recent indulgences, these men had tried to take things into their own hands. Whatever their story was, they would not be sharing it at evening meal, for the drums began their steady beat yet again. Their warrants and sentences were read, but then a swift wind carried across the platform. Their robes were ruffled as a blinding light ripped through the crowd. I, myself, fell backward as I stumbled in fear. Either magic or devil work I cannot say, but in that flash of energy two bodies went missing. Six remained, swinging lifeless as the crowd shrieked in disbelief at the spectacle, and the strange orange and yellow glow faded away slowly..."

Harris stood off to the side, allowing the others a better look. They read the article and one by one, the realization of their narrow escape from death hung high over their heads. Then the loss of a brother, close friends, and a lover all brought tears to their eyes.

"I don't understand." Leah cried, hoping an explanation of what had really happened would soon be provided. She looked around, "What happened to Ben?"

Harris ignored Leah's question, attempting to make a logical deduction first. He looked at Sal. "Listen, we've traveled back through time once. I bet we're sometime in the future now, probably not too long since we actually left, or even maybe at the same time, just a different place. Let's try and find out where and when we are."

Leah cringed at the statement. She had absolutely no idea what Harris was talking about. Another wave of tears came.

Sal nodded. "Yeah, good idea. I think you're on to something."

Nelson remained quiet, placing a reassuring hand on Leah's shoulder. He then looked at Harris and Sal to get their attention. "Leah." He cleared his throat. "There is much for us to explain. I know that this does not make any sense at all to you, but I know that there is something we can do."

Leah began sniffling so loudly that Nelson thought it best to wait for her to calm down before speaking again. She finally nodded for him to continue. "Our rescue lies within this crimson journal," he paused, pulling out the journal from his breast pocket, "upon these gold medallions around your necks and lastly, inside that magical staff." He looked into the display, noticing the precious stone glittering in mockery.

His fist broke through the glass. Blood quickly welled upon his knuckles as he removed the three-foot-long cursed staff from the display. In the distance a security alarm went off at the main security desk, its sound filling the grand halls of the museum.

The End